The Tale of Outh'n Durr

Tales of Y'Dahnndrya, Volume 5

Robin McElveen

Published by MKRM Author, 2022.

THE TALE OF OUTH'N DURR

First edition. June 30, 2022.

Copyright © 2022 Robin McElveen.

ISBN: 978-1732263260

Written by Robin McElveen.

Table of Contents

For Caleb, one of the quirkiest and most talented misfits I've ever had the honor to work with. Remember who you are, and Whose you are. May God grant you the desires of your heart.

And to all the misfits among misfits like me. Remember you are not alone.

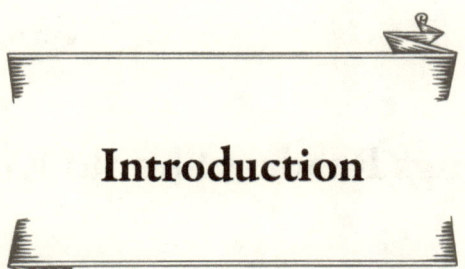

Introduction

The Tale of Outh'n Durr tells the story of a man who is a misfit among his people through no real fault of his own. Sometimes, people are just flat-out mean because they're miserable and want everyone around them to be miserable, too. That's not how people <u>should</u> behave and certainly not how God wants us to act, but some people reject God and the teachings in the Bible in favor of self. Anytime we put ourselves in front of everyone else and attempt to put ourselves in the position of God in our lives, bad things happen. Why? Because we are not gods and we are certainly not The Almighty King of Kings and Lord of Lords. We are not perfect and can never achieve that without the help of the only perfect being who exists.

This is a work of fiction. Any resemblance to any of my fellow human beings is purely coincidental.

Things Readers Should Know

Y'Dahnndrya is a world with two large continents and many islands (so far). She orbits twin suns. Her traveling companions are five moons. Time flows differently on Y'Dahnndrya. Six seasons (dahlsikin; sing., dahlsik) comprising three months (minsikin; sing., minsik) each make up one Y'Dahnndryan year, called a tsimik (pl., tsimikin). The minsik cycle follows the largest moon. Each month comprises four weeks, which are each nine days long. The word <u>nainda</u> is used for one or more Y'Dahnndryan weeks. One Y'Dahnndryan year is 648 days long. A day is often referred to as a dawning, while a night is sometimes called a dusking.

For more information, I've provided an index, a pronunciation guide, and a glossary which all wait patiently at the end of the story for those who crave more knowledge of my book world.

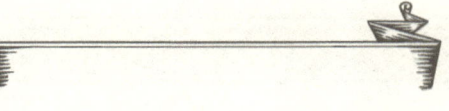

So Let's Begin

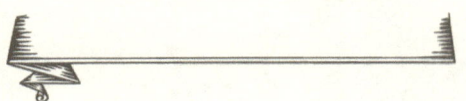

Dear Reader, thank you for picking up this book and giving it a chance. It is my fervent prayer that the contents enrich your life. If you take one thing away from the reading of it, may it be that being determined to do the right thing, despite how people treat you, will pay off. But sometimes, it happens in ways you least expect.

Outh'n Durr is a complex character and was quite difficult to write. He's still learning about himself and how he's going to interact with his world and the people who share it with him. I wrote this little novella as an introduction to the second book of the Children of Y'Dahnndrya series, <u>Surge</u>, which is coming soon. To be honest, I tried writing a shorter story, but Outh'n wasn't having it. I do hope I have given enough closure so readers can choose whether to read book two without feeling cheated.

I like to include a verse of scripture with each of my stories, though the novels themselves aren't necessarily inspirational. I hope this verse will encourage you.

<u>"They will fight against you, but they will not prevail against you; for I am with you," says [Adonai],"to rescue you." - Jeremiah 1:19 World English Bible[1]</u>

1. http://ebible.org/study/

The Tale of Outh'n Durr by Robin McElveen ©2019, October
Cover page by Melody R Kittles ©2019, October

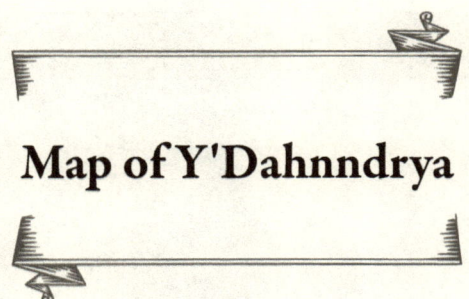

Map of Y'Dahnndrya

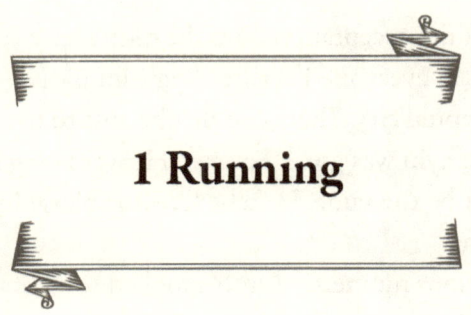

1 Running

There. Gasping, Outh'n Durr raced for the animal den he knew was empty and big enough to hide him from his pursuers. Questions flickered through his mind with each pounding footfall.

Why were they after him? How could his own people believe he would hurt the only person who'd chosen to befriend him? Why him? Was it so bad to want to be part of their fun? He just wanted to be accepted. Why did Tugansol, the Life Giver, seem to want Outh'n's life snuffed out?

He'd long left the villagers behind. Outh'n might be outwardly imperfect with one eye crossed, a scar through the eyebrow above that eye, and a slightly crooked nose marring the symmetry of what would otherwise be a handsome face. But he prided himself on figuring out how to work around the vision impairment and had learned to live with the face that stared back at him from the surface of the village pond.

What he lacked in physical beauty, he made up for with speed and agility. After winning a few awards for speed and archery, the villagers actively began discouraging him from participating. Kurg'l, the son of a village Senya, wouldn't stand for anyone besting him in any competition.

So Outh'n had focused on the other thing he was good at, working with his hands. And it had paid off. His apprenticeship request to the Oxyl Glashiin Workers set out a minsik ago, and Outh'n had opened the reply only yesterdawn with nervous fingers. He'd whooped aloud when he read of the acceptance. Now, he didn't have to wait to get out of Prichud, where everyone kept holding him back. All he had to do was get to the capital city. They wouldn't be able to touch him in Oxyl.

But now Alanyin was gone. Forever. He was being blamed, and his life would never be the same. He'd be Creator-blessed if he lived to see the next dawning.

Taking precious moments, Outh'n looked for a branch of pungent miklanin. Spotting a shrub beside the path, he snapped a branch free and crushed some leaves. He stashed a few in his pocket. Foul-smelling, but it would disguise his scent from a hunting pack of wuve, as well as brush away evidence of his passage. He retraced his steps to a stream he'd jumped to reach the shrub and began erasing his scent by traveling up the stream quickly and quietly for a suitable distance. When he judged he'd gone far enough, he pulled some leaves from his pocket and scattered them on the ground. He brushed over them with his wet boots, then scattered a few more leaves as he continued toward his chosen haven.

The slowness ate at his already fractured psyche and he couldn't decide which urging to listen to. In the end, he worked steadily, reminding himself it was better this way. Whether the villagers caught him here or at his hiding place, the result would be the same. At least this way, he had a better chance of surviving. He worked on with renewed determination.

After what seemed forever, the miklanin shrub which covered the opening of the abandoned den came into view. Outh'n was never more happy for his thin, flexible frame. He'd had to hide in the cramped space many times before. The only difference this time was how much it would cost him if the villagers found him. His life, such as it was, hung in the balance.

Long moments passed, and exhaustion overcame the youngling. He fell asleep to whispers drifting through the turning leaves as a cool breeze reminded all who felt it of the changing dahlsik.

"WE'RE CLOSE. I KNOW it."

Kurg'l's strident voice cut through the murk of Outh'n's sleep. He tensed and waited.

"How do you know, Kurg'l?" Deil was there, too. Their babei sat on the village council, allowing them to get away with much more than they should have.

How he wished Alanyin was here! Tears stung his eyes at the memory of her broken body on the ground at his feet. He'd tried to catch her. He was so fast. Why couldn't he catch her? Only the day before, she'd spoken to him of Kurg'l's disregard for her honor. Outh'n couldn't help thinking the misbegotten son-of-a-whe'evet had only treated her so badly because he knew his actions would anger Outh'n. The blame was his and his alone. Everything bad that happened to her was only because she wanted to be his friend and, fool that he was, he couldn't say no.

He blinked away the tears and tensed as the sweep and crackle of dead leaves grew louder. They were closer than they should be. How? Did he miss something? Leave a stray footprint? Forget to snap a hanging twig?

"I know it's around here somewhere. The misfigured son-of-a-silti hides around here often."

"Follow him a lot, eiya?"

"Herd your own bix'n, Deil," the menace in Kurg'l's voice was as threatening as glashiin shards. His voice, just like the shards, dug in, promising infection and a slow, painful death. "You could easily be in his place. Wasn't it your voice startled the maid?"

"How do you know that?"

"I know a lot of things." Kurg'l's laugh was one of the most unpleasant things Outh'n had ever known.

Icy cold flooded Outh'n, starting in his heart. He hadn't caused Alanyin's fall. It was Deil. And now his friend was gone forever. Fury clawed its way out from within the deepest part of him, blinding Outh'n to his own danger. Under normal circumstances, he was well aware they'd outmatch him in an outright brawl, mostly because he couldn't bring himself to fight dirty. When he tried, he botched it and cheating always ate at his sense of self-respect. Too, he didn't want to sabotage any blessing Tugansol might wish to bestow on him.

None of that mattered now. He shot out of his hole among the boulders and tree roots, catching Deil off guard.

A bark of victorious laughter barely cut through the berserk haze in his mind. "It was you? How could you? Why?" Outh'n punctuated each question with a swing at Deil's side, stomach, or face, wherever he could find an opening.

So focused on the rival facing him, Outh'n forgot all about his other opponent. Kurg'l worked his way around the scuffling pair and picked up a chunk of stone.

Pain flared at the back of Outh'n's head and he knew no more.

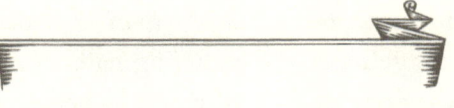

2 Imprisoned

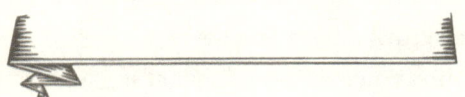

When he came to, darkness surrounded him. Outh'n's head pounded and his neck and shoulder ached. Cold, hard dirt made an uncomfortable bed. He lay puzzled for only a moment before sitting up in realization. Grabbing his head with both hands, he groaned as nausea threatened to overcome him. He was in the village kaila, awaiting the judgment of the council. Sorrow filled his heart as memories flooded his mind.

Scrabbling and scratching emanated from the shadows and he called out, "Who's there?"

"Outh'n? You're awake?" The whisper was faint, but he thought it must be his sadau.

"What are you doing here, Ailiin? It's dangerous. Go home." He tried to sound gruff, but his throbbing headache weakened the effect.

"You don't belong here." She ignored his command and continued. "Why would I not try to help?" she insisted. "Besides, Moyri sent you some food. The council forbade it but you know how Moyri is."

Outh'n allowed one corner of his mouth to rise in a weak grin. She couldn't see it, anyway. "Moyri's not the only one."

A soft chuckle rippled through the gloom. "I'll leave this by the door then. I can't reach much further than that."

"How long have I been here?"

"A dawning and a dusking."

Outh'n's eyebrows rose. "So long?"

"There's some argument about Alanyin's fall being accidental or not. They're still arguing at the gathering hall." A soft snort directed Outh'n toward the door to his prison and he began the torturous trek toward sustenance. The scent of Moyri's baked sweet buns and roasted meat hit him suddenly. His stomach growled, urging him to hurry should the guard return and take it away.

"Outh'n," Ailiin's voice trembled, "what will we do if they determine it wasn't an accident? You could die." The grate rattled thinly. She must have reached through, but Outh'n's vision was still not as clear as it should be. Having his one reliable eye blurry hampered him. How hard had Kurg'l hit him?

"I can't see you, Ailiin," he murmured as he reached out one hand toward her voice. Her delicate fingers grasped his long, calloused ones tightly. "I don't know what will happen. No one but Tugansol does, and the Giver of Life seems bent on taking mine away." He hated the bitter tinge ruining his attempt to soothe Ailiin's worry.

"Don't talk that way about Tugansol. You will certainly bring holy wrath down upon you, and maybe on your family who loves you, too." She abruptly released his hand. "Did you do what they're accusing you of? Is this why you're so certain of a guilty verdict?"

He shook his head instinctively and groaned as his wound reminded him viciously of its presence. "I did not," he whispered brokenly. "She was my only friend. I would never, never hurt her Ailiin. Never. How could you even ask that?"

Moyri's sweet bun turned to ashes in his suddenly dry mouth. He could barely swallow the hard lump. Resolute, he pushed past the discomfort and forced it down, knowing it was likely his last meal.

Outh'n heard her braids brush against her clothing as she nodded. "I believe you. I know Moyri believes in your innocence. Babeiya speaks for you even now."

"What are you not telling me?" he asked during a tense pause.

"They are the only ones on your side, Outh'n. Kurg'l and Deil both speak against you, along with their parents. Alanyin's babei also speaks fervently against you, swearing on Tugansol's life-giving breath." She huffed. "The council of Senya didn't like that bit at all."

"You'd better go back," Outh'n swallowed hard. Had all hope really vanished? "Go quickly, before the guard finds you here. Take this," he passed the cloth which had wrapped the meager meal back through the grate. "Tell Moyri I thank her for sending my favorite sweet buns. Tell both her and Babeiya I love them and thank them for believing in me."

"Don't give up, Iyaba," she urged as she rose. "Tugansol cannot be ready to call you to Zoleta already."

"Perhaps you're right." He hadn't the heart to tell her he expected to be sent to Surteit instead, to be tortured with pain and darkness for all eternity. "Go now, before they miss you."

The soft scruff of boot-clad feet on dirt faded into the distance, much like Outh'n's hope of justice.

"OUTH'N?" THE SWEET sound rang in his ears. "Outh'n, where are you? Won't you come out and talk?" He hesitated. He'd heard such urgings before and they'd gained him only pain and humiliation when he dared to hope.

"I promise," the melodious voice continued, "I'm not like them. I don't like how they treat you. Please, come out."

Silence filled the green meadow until the birds once again took up their songs. Thinking she'd left, Outh'n crept out of hiding.

"There you are!"

Her sudden words startled him and he spun too quickly, losing his balance and tumbling over into a heap. She giggled. He waited, expecting to hear more jeers and laughter at his expense. A quick scan of the area showed she was truly alone. He marveled at the fact that someone wanted to talk to him after all this time. He'd lived for ten tsimikin and for too many of them had tried in vain to make friends in his small village. Was his patience finally rewarded? Had Tugansol answered his prayers?

"Greetings," said the small girl perched atop a boulder. "My name's Alanyin."

"I'm Outh'n Durr," he said stupidly, then ducked his chin as heat flooded his neck and cheeks.

She giggled behind her hand. "I know. I called out for you, remember?"

He nodded, struck mute by her joy.

"What are you doing out here?"

"Hiding." This Alanyin was nosy. Outh'n wasn't sure how he felt about all her questions.

"Why?"

"You know why."

She shook her head. "I know you hide from the others, and I don't blame you. I'm new here, but I saw what they did to you the day my family came to this village. What I mean is, why aren't you doing something you enjoy?"

"They won't let me do those things if they find me." He shook his head in annoyance and frustration roughened his tone. "And if by some miracle I actually complete a piece and they find me then, they smash my work and it's all for nothing."

Tears pooled in her brilliant blue eyes. She shoved wayward tendrils of golden brown hair back from her face, but the breeze blew it back. She ignored it and said, "I'm so sorry, Outh'n. We'll find a way for you to have some fun. I'll help you."

That was how it had begun, his friendship with Alanyin. He'd thought to ask her to bond with him one dawning. With the promise of an apprenticeship, the time had loomed nearer. Now they'd dashed that hope as easily and completely as when they ruined his glashiin work all those tsimikin ago. He couldn't believe six tsimikin had already passed. A tear rolled unchecked down his cheek, followed by another, then several more. He didn't even bother to wipe them away. What did it matter, after all? Tugansol must've given up on him. He'd be dead soon and no one would care but his parents and sadau.

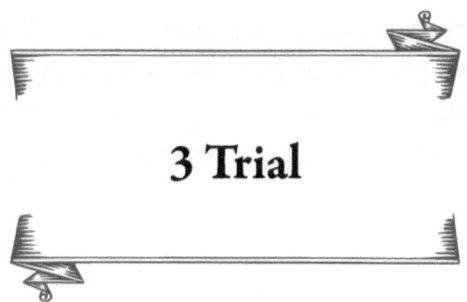

3 Trial

When he was certain Ailiin was away, Outh'n released howls and curses, exorcising his hatred and frustration in the shadows. Scratchy throat, paired with the pounding headache, punished him for the reckless overflow.

"My apologies, great Tugansol," he rasped. He'd sound like a raug'l for a while. "But it's hard to think there can be any good in losing my best friend, the woman I loved. Why did you snatch her away? And why allow the others to threaten me because she died?" He ran his hands through his hair and groaned. "I've done nothing wrong. They've treated me horribly before, but this? I'm so stupid to have ever hoped my village would stand up for me after all that's come before," he murmured.

Silence haunted his ears between the swishing surges of his own heartbeat. He snorted at his pitiful behavior. As if Tugansol would suddenly speak to him, the least desirable person in Prichud! The Life-Giver didn't appreciate a prideful heart. He shook his head, slowly this time, mindful of the throbbing.

KEYS JANGLED AGAINST the lock, startling Outh'n from a fitful doze. Icy dread flooded his stomach and he clenched his jaw in preparation. Moving wouldn't be pleasant. If they were opening the door, judgment had been determined. Whether or not he was ready, it was time to hear the verdict.

"Come on, you son-of-a-silti," the guard cursed at him from the door, blinding him with a blazing torch. "Come on, I say! You're in luck. Looks as if the council's letting you off lightly, though I can't figure out why. Neither can most of the village." He spat on the dirt near Outh'n's feet. "You're the worst kind of bistarra, Outh'n Durr," he sneered. This curse stabbed at Outh'n's heart. He'd often wondered if he actually belonged to his parents or if they'd found him abandoned somewhere. "Anyone who'd kill a friend deserves to die in my mind." The guard shook his head and turned sideways to allow Outh'n to pass in front of him. "Now. Let's go," he pushed Outh'n's shoulder as he growled, "Move your feet, trash."

Outh'n stumbled awkwardly to the wooden door of the kaila. He couldn't see it yet, but the thought of it beckoned him to freedom. He just didn't know which kind of freedom it would be. Every step he took shuddered through him, shards of pain radiating from his head wound. He tried to focus on the guard's words, wondering at the sickening hint of hope. Had they cleared him of all wrong? Did someone besides his family believe he was telling the truth?

His ankle gave way as he stepped into a dip. Catching himself proved more difficult with a staff prodding him onward, but he managed it. The primal growl of pain leapt out of his throat before he could clamp his lips to trap it. A sharp rap to his shoulders with the flat of the staff punctuated the guard's clipped rebuke and propelled him on. A brilliant, silver line close to the floor confused Outh'n at first, until he realized the door was near.

As they reached the ray of questionable hope, it widened on one side. The door squawked on its old hinges and the searing light and warmth of the mid-dawning suns lanced his eyes. He'd thought the torch was bad, but now he cowered as the cheery rays lanced his eyes. Instinct squeezed his eyes shut, strengthening the throbbing behind his right ear and at his temples. He whimpered and gripped his head once again, willing the pain to cease. His eyes streamed and burned, his feet stumbling along the uneven path he could barely see. Through the ceaseless torment, he barely registered the strikes on his legs and back.

"That's enough, Garrik," a gruff, unfamiliar voice reprimanded the guard.

"But, Senya, he isn't— " a resounding crunch followed by a grunt cut the guard's complaint off.

"I said that's enough. He can barely walk as it is."

"As you say, Senya," Garrik's muffled voice moved as he stumbled off to one side. The guard hovered near enough to catch Outh'n if he tried to run, though the younger man shuddered at the thought of it. Outh'n wasn't going anywhere they didn't force him to go.

A gentle hand clasped his shoulder. He jerked, expecting the sharpness the guard had displayed. "Come Outh'n Durr. I will escort you into the gathering hall."

Outh'n stood taller, though his hands still cradled his head. The throbbing had increased, and it seemed his head might roll off his shoulders. "Thank you," he murmured and waited.

"I am Bazhbet Mehya of Chefvna, called in for special deliberation on your behalf. Your parents must love you a great deal to send so far away for help. Their actions convinced me of your innocence."

Outh'n nodded, then winced, berating himself for his stupidity. "Yes," he croaked, "I love them, too, Senya." So his parents sent away for a Senya who would not cower before the village council members who hated him. "But the real reason is most probably because my accusers are sons of men on the council."

"So that's the way of it, is it?" A gruff, mirthless laugh rumbled through the air. "Well, we shall see how this goes, then, youngling. Come on," he gently nudged Outh'n's shoulder and walked slightly behind him, allowing Outh'n to set the pace.

A new kind of torture it was. He didn't want to be here, didn't want to face all the villagers who were surely filling the gathering hall to the rafters. Their jeers and snubs were difficult to hear on the best of dawnings. He trudged forward, reluctant, yet knowing there was no way out. Garryk's thudding steps followed on the opposite side at his back. He knew the guard would take any opportunity to thwack him again.

Outh'n stumbled and pitched forward. A vice clamped around his bicep and kept him from plowing face first into the hard-packed dirt path. "Thank you, Senya," he replied dutifully.

A grunt was the only reply, so he started forward again. Cold stones piled up in his belly before melting to burning lava as he neared the side door. Maybe Tugansol would take him quickly, for at least the Creator could see the truth about matters. Surely, the very Breath of Life would be merciful and steal the breath bestowed upon Outh'n before the guilty ones could.

4 Banished

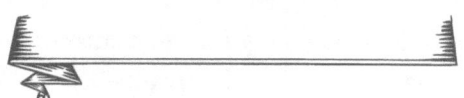

O uth'n should've known. Tugansol wasn't listening to his prayers
lately. His sudden hope must have come from the desperate need
for relief, the unrelenting assault on his temples and eyes. Surely, that
accounted for his stupidity.

The council, with stringent urging from Senya Mehya, who sided
with him, determined he didn't deserve to die. No. Instead, the life of a
wanderer awaited him. He was now a tiav'yag, an exile. Once the brand
marked his left cheek, everyone would see his shame. The broken circle
with three wisps of smoke would be evidence to all of his failure to
remain loyal to his people and to Tugansol.

Outh'n finally accepted that he might never understand why he was
the scapegoat. A tiav'yag had no home in Shinnoah. There was only one
thing wanderers could do for certain — walk.

"You must work your way south to Mt. Charan," Bazhbet had urged
him as he walked Outh'n to the border of Prichud. "Seth Yi'in will
guide you, once you show your mettle." A chuckle emanated from the
man's chest. "He's a funny little man, for certain. Tugansol chose a
strange Guardian for our people."

Outh'n had stared at him, confused. "You're sending me to
Tugansol's servant?" At the Senya's nod, he asked, "Why? Tugansol
hasn't heard my prayers for a long time." He hung his head. "Why would
the Breath of Life show care for me now? My own village rejects me."
He glared up at Bazhbet and insisted, "I just can't believe the Holy One
cares at all."

The Senya was silent for so long, Outh'n fidgeted and dug into the earth with the toe of his boot. When he finally spoke, Bazhbet startled the youngling with his rough whisper.

"Outh'n Durr, never doubt that Tugansol has spared your life for a reason. There is something you must do and only you can complete this task. It is also apparent to me and anyone else with eyes that you won't be able to accomplish that task if you stay in Prichud. Otherwise," he shrugged and grinned like a wuveia on the hunt, "we both know the verdict would have been much different."

After thinking over the man's words, Outh'n nodded reluctantly. He wasn't sure he believed Tugansol had spared him from much. The life of a tiav'yag was the most difficult one which existed in Shinnoah. He'd only seen a wanderer once. The people had thrown rotten food and hurled harsher insults than he had ever received. That day, he'd been thankful Tugansol had at least spared him that humiliation. In the end, the woman had fled his village, her shrieking curses echoing back like the harsh cries of the mountain-dwelling whe'evet.

Outh'n shook his head again. "As you say, Senya," he mumbled and rolled his eyes, resulting in sending a shooting pain back through his head. "Eiya," he groaned when Bazhbet flicked Outh'n's right temple. The glare he directed at the man resulted in a rich chuckle.

But Bazhbet wasn't unkind. "You may think this is no great thing Tugansol has allowed. But I promise you, while there is life, hope remains."

"Hope for what, Senya?" Outh'n threw up his hands. "My family home is the only haven I know, the only place I received love and kindness. And now, because of an tragedy I had nothing to do with, the people who've taken away everything else in my life have barred me from the one thing I thought I'd never lose. How can you say there's hope?" His eyes burned, anger fueled with sorrow. Red-tinged eyes zeroed in on the Senya. He was aware his behavior wasn't the right way to thank his rescuer. Neither did he want the Senya to hate him like everyone else. But it was hard to look with favor upon the messenger of such dire news.

"Come," Bazhbet urged him toward a wooden bench near the path. "Come and sit with me for a moment." The faint music of glashiin wind singers clinked in the distance. He grinned despite the gloomy future ahead of him and wondered if the chime was one of his.

"Something amuses you, Outh'n Durr?"

Outh'n nodded. "They hate me so much. I still don't know why. It can't all be because of this." He gestured toward his lazy eye, turning it away from Bazhbet as he continued. "But they buy my glashiin work. All of them. They don't know it, of course, but every one of them has something I made. They paid me, and a pretty shinma, too. So, yes, that amuses me, Senya." He ran one hand through his hair, spiking it, and chuckled wryly. "The only downside is that I'll never see their faces when they find out."

"You work with glashiin?" Wonder colored his question.

Outh'n nodded. "My yuenda said I could get a job with the Hatw'n Guild."

Bazhbet whistled and shook his head. When Outh'n didn't speak again, he said, "Well, that won't happen now, but at least you have the skill. You could find it useful."

"How?" Outh'n threw up his hands in frustration. "How will I earn money for the tools and supplies I need? I have nothing, Senya. And my parents have only enough to feed themselves and Ailiin. I can't and won't ask for their help. They've done enough, endured more than they should've for me." He rose and stretched carefully, thankful he didn't have to go back to the dark hole they'd kept him in before his trial.

"Yes, we must continue." Bazhbet also rose. "You'll need to say goodbye to your family."

Outh'n eyed the Senya, one eyebrow raised. "How is that possible, Senya? And why are you even talking to me now? Haven't they set my punishment?"

The Senya nodded. "It has. But just because you wear a tiav'yag brand, that's no reason for me to treat you as less than human. People choose to treat the wanderers as they will. No laws protect them, but neither are there laws to prohibit kindness toward them. The brand simply means you won't find it as easy to settle into a home or earn your keep. Everything that was difficult before will be even more difficult for you."

Outh'n stared at Bazhbet's solemn but gentle eyes, finally nodding resolutely. "I understand, Senya. I must somehow learn to charm others, a skill, it seems, I've lacked from the dawning of my birth." He grimaced. "You make things sound so easy."

"Come on, youngling." Senya Mehya chuckled again. "We both have long trails to travel."

Outh'n would have trudged, but villagers cowered in the shadows of buildings and trees along the path. If it wasn't for his giant rescuer, Outh'n was sure they would try to kill him. Yes, his sentence could have been worse but, by the Holy Breath! He couldn't see how death was worse than never again seeing the only people who loved him.

5 Wanderer

Outh'n jerked awake suddenly as something scratched the back of his hand. Yesterdawn, as the suns sank below the horizon and the shadows of the forest had grown, he'd found a tree whose roots had kindly created a comfortable nest. Mazh and dry leaves lined the bottom, and the underbrush surrounding the trunk concealed the space from the casual passerby. Wedging himself between two branching roots and using his pack as a pillow, he'd gotten the deepest sleep he'd had since leaving Prichud.

Until now. He carefully checked his knuckles. No broken skin or blood, not even a small red streak or dot, met his careful inspection. He looked around, inspecting the darker spots within the confines of his nest. A soot-black ball of fur about half the size of his palm caught his eye. He reached for it.

"So you're the culprit, eiya?" Outh'n smiled indulgently, stretching muscles he hadn't used since before his exile three nainda past. Bizhals were one of the few beasts of Shinnoah whose personalities matched their looks. Fuzzy, ultra-soft fur covered their small, round bodies. They walked on four tiny feet, their toes tipped with rounded claws built for digging through the dirt and leaves to uncover the insects they feasted on. Two round, brilliant blue eyes met his own golden brown ones, and the creature purred.

"At least I know you didn't intend harm. Are you hunting, little one?" Outh'n lowered his cupped hands so the bizhal could step out if it wished. It stayed, waving its two feathered antennae as if in question.

"Oh, I'm just passing through." Outh'n grimaced. "I have little choice, really. I'm an outcast." When the beastie made no move but gazed at him steadily, Outh'n spoke again. "You don't care, do you?" he smiled gratefully as he continued, "But I can't take you with me, little one. If anyone knew you befriended me, they'd try to take you away or harm you. You're better off without me."

As if it understood, the creature crept slowly off of Outh'n's palms. It felt nothing like the scrape that had awakened him. He watched as it bumbled back to the place where he'd picked it up. Stopping there for just a moment, it picked up something in its mouth, then bumbled away. A glimpse was all Outh'n got of its prey, but he paled at the telltale aurora of a kinzhik's thin, iridescent wings.

"Thank you, little friend," Outh'n whispered faintly. If it had stung him, there would be little hope of surviving the poison. Bile rose in his throat. Perhaps Tugansol watched over him despite his wavering faith. He offered a quick prayer of thanks just in case the Creator was listening.

Outh'n stood once the bizhal was gone and brushed himself free from leaves and twigs. His shoulders protested as he lifted his pack and shrugged it into place. Taking a deep breath, he set out for the path, fighting his way through the underbrush. His stomach reminded him he should eat something, but this place wasn't far enough away from the main road. Wild berries or nuts would have to do, overripe and hard to find, though they may be.

A sudden clamor from behind him, toward the main trail, halted him. Halfway through a patch of prickly underbrush, he had no choice but to duck into it, knowing well the scratches that would decorate the few bare patches of skin he'd not been able to cover. One thorn raked over the still tender flesh of his cheek where the branding iron had sent him into blessed oblivion. He hissed but clamped his jaws together quickly. Hopefully, he was far enough from the trail that whoever was passing by would remain oblivious to his presence.

It didn't seem possible, but instead of passing, the clamor seemed to move further away from him. What in the name of the Life-giving Breath sent them away? Considering the reasons a caravan would turn aside to another path didn't encourage him. The few he could think of had quite efficient teeth and claws. To send them running so quickly, the options were fewer still.

It couldn't be whe'evet. They stayed in the mountain ranges, only coming down to the valleys during extreme storms. Bah'riim? He was too far west under normal circumstances, though one may have strayed from their usual hunting grounds. He shook his head.

Wuveia. It had to be. And this close, the pack would already have his scent. They'd probably picked up his conversation with the bizhal moments ago and were biding their time. Deciding it was now or never, Outh'n made his move and rose from the thorny thicket. Coming to his knees, he met the golden-eyed glare of one of the beasts.

Dear Tugansol in Zoleta, it was massive! He'd never seen one up close, only from a distance as he'd watched over his babeiya's cattle. The domesticated wuve, relatives of these forest dwellers, never grew this big. But their presence on a farm seemed to discourage their larger kyn from feasting on the pastured animals.

Outh'n sat back on his heels, resigned to a fast, bloody death. Shaking violently, he closed his eyes and bared his throat. If he made himself an easy target, maybe death would be swifter, less painful. He'd had enough of pain over the course of his life and what did he have to live for, anyway? He was more than ready to die.

6 Acceptance

Snuffling startled him and little puffs of air danced over Outh'n's face, moving from ear to ear, from crown to chin. He opened his eyes to watch as the wuveia continued its inspection from his neck to his knees. When it finished, it sat and stared at Outh'n.

How long he sat with the creature was a mystery, but the stinging in his legs warned him to move soon. Would the great beast attack when he obeyed the frantic urging of his legs? Perhaps slight movements would be best. He opened one palm and offered it to the wuveia, facing up. The beast, dark brown dotted with gold and cream flecks, bent its head to sniff tentatively at the offered appendage.

The cool touch of its snout startled Outh'n and the sound that came from his throat sounded so fearful he was ashamed. The animal obviously meant no harm. "I'm sorry, friend," he murmured. "Stories of the fierceness of your kind have spread far." He reached a shaking hand toward the wuveia and tentatively touched the space between its shaggy, pointed ears. The fur was coarse and full of seed burrs. But he managed a good scratch there and then behind its ears. As surely as the rising of the suns, its tongue was soon lolling happily.

Outh'n smiled. He'd lost his best friend, but Tugansol smiled on him for the second time this dawning. "Will you walk with me, friend?" he asked as he rose to his feet, reached out to the nearest tree for support. He growled in pain as blood raced toward his feet. For a while, he concentrated on each breath.

When he felt his legs would support him, he headed for the main path. His new friend would have none of it, though, steering him deeper into the forest.

"This way, eiya?" He looked into the wuveia's eyes and shrugged. "Alright, friend. I'll trust you. All others have either betrayed me or are out of my reach. If you feel you must leave in the end, I won't hold it against you. I thank you for your presence now, though. Being a tiav'yag is a lonely existence." He followed the beast's lead and kept as close as he dared.

When he fell behind, which he was prone to do — Bazhbet Mehya and his own moyri had stuffed his pack full of supplies — the wuveia waited for him to catch up. They traveled in this way for the better part of the dawning. As dusking crept across the sky-dome and the tree shadows grew long and blended with each other, they came to a rocky den. His new friend alerted the others of his kind with a series of guttural whines and chuffs. Outh'n wondered if this would be an ending or a beginning.

An older, graying member of the pack loped toward Outh'n, who stood his ground and held his breath. He'd thought his friend was huge! This one stood eye-level with him. It repeated the sniffing ritual, this time punctuated with a beast kiss, which left a trail of cold saliva on his branded cheek. The others of the pack drew nearer, each of them sniffing at him curiously, interjecting more grunts and whines. He stood still, waiting patiently until the inspection of the new being in their midst was complete.

When all returned to their rest, Outh'n removed his pack and carefully set it down. He unbuckled the flap and rummaged around inside until he found the packet of jerked meat his moyri had included. Pulling the small bag open at the mouth, he offered pieces to each of them. The small bits of meat were gone in seconds. He wondered whether they would fight each other or attack him to get more of the food, but they simply ate each offering and sat quietly. Some drifted off to sleep, while others seemed to keep watch. A few slunk off into the forest. The muffled sounds which echoed back told a clear enough tale as they drifted through the trees. It must be their mating season.

Outh'n couldn't help but wonder if there would ever be a chance for him to find a life-mate. Who'd have him now, branded as he was? Another tiav'yag? But could he trust any of them? He'd done nothing to warrant his mark, but that wouldn't be true of all the others. How could he tell the good from the bad? These questions and more thrummed a discordant lullaby which sent him into a restless sleep that night.

An insistent nudge on the small of his back woke him before the suns had risen. His new friend was most insistent and not about to be ignored. "Alright, alright. I'm getting up." He grumbled as he sat up and stretched. When he rubbed the sleep from his eyes, he noticed the pack standing at attention. A series of harsh growls punctuated with snapping jaws sent them scurrying in several directions.

Outh'n grabbed for his pack. He'd forgotten to buckle the flap last night and a few items flew free in his haste. Muttering under his breath, he left them. Maybe he could replace them and maybe not. It didn't matter. His life was definitely more important than whatever had flown free, even food. He'd learned to be resourceful since his trial, anyway.

A brown flash up ahead showed his friend dashing into a heavy patch of shrubs. He followed, heedless of what lay ahead, only caring what might happen if he got left behind. The heavy pack nestled awkwardly in his arms. He hoped to avoid more spillage and that slowed him down, but he put on an extra burst of speed, reaching the bushes just in time. He took a few precious moments to hide himself among them. A single broken branch would ruin everything. Then the waiting game began.

Voices drifted to him, the words he could pick out filling him with anger and frustration. A cold nose touched his knuckles in warning. He forced his muscles to relax and urged his ears to listen harder.

"But Kurg'l," Deil whined, "we've been following his trail for so long now. Why haven't we caught up?"

"Who says we haven't?" Outh'n's chest tightened as he held his breath. They must've spotted his scattered belongings.

"What is that?" The annoyance in Deil's voice disappeared.

"Looks like jerked meat in this one. And," Silence fell over the clearing while Kurg'l inspected his other find. "This one's full of dried berries."

"Hey, look at this." Deil's excitement was a tangible thing and couldn't bode well for Outh'n. He glanced at his friend, whose shoulders twitched beside him, and laid a calming hand on the one nearest him. The magnificent beast stilled.

Kurg'l's cackle of glee was the most unpleasant sound Outh'n had ever heard. "We're going back, Deil. See here?"

"Wuveia?" Outh'n could hear the taint of fear in the younger man's voice.

"What are you afraid of? They've overtaken Outh'n. He's scrawny, but surely they've had their fill. So, we're leaving. If they've gotten him, and it looks like they have, then they stole my prize from me. The result's the same, though."

Footsteps strong and sure paced away from the shrubs where Outh'n and his friend hid. Even though their voices were fading, their words came back clear enough.

"Outh'n Durr was a craven misfit and only Tugansol knows why Alanyin chose him over me or you." He snorted in disgust. "Why the Holy Breath would grant him such speed and accuracy, and gift him with an illustrious apprenticeship is a mystery which will remain hidden. Blessing sure seemed to rest on him. At least now I'm rid of him and can get on with my suit of Ailiin. She will pay for the trouble he's caused me. By the time she understands what's going on, it'll be too late."

Tears flowed down Outh'n's cheeks unheeded. All this time, Kurg'l's only aim had been to annihilate him. Outh'n finally understood. The desire to receive the violet ribbon and triple flame medal might have been the truth, but Kurg'l hated him, truly hated him. Why? Outh'n had thought his heart couldn't break any further, but when he realized there was nothing he could've done to change the current outcome, he felt an intact shard shatter.

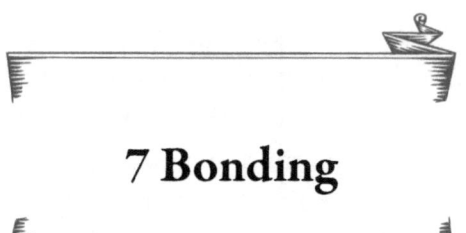

7 Bonding

How long he sat in the shrubs, he didn't know. His friend had ceased the gentle nudging to nip at his ears. Almost, he wished his friend would kill him; almost allowed self-pity to ruin any hope of helping Ailiin.

"What can I do, Friend? My sadau is in danger if I can't get a message to her. But who will carry a tiav'yag's message?" He dropped his head into his hands and grumbled. The next nip took a bit of skin with it and had him rising to his feet with a cry of surprise.

"Alright," he growled as he frowned at the wuveia who stood staring at him with an approving grin, a jaunty tilt of his head easing Outh'n's ire. "I wish I knew what to call you."

"Oowah." The beast uttered a guttural reply.

Outh'n's jaw dropped. "Did," he started, his jaw working to form words, "did you just answer me?"

The beast's head dipped once.

"By the Holy Breath," he murmured in awe, receiving another nip for his irreverence. "Ouch!"

Oowah snuffed and snorted.

"Alright. I'll mind my words." A sound, half-gasp, half-chuckle, punctuated his promise.

Oowah nodded again once.

"I need to find someone who'll send a message home for me. I have to warn Ailiin."

His friend stepped closer and danced nimbly on his front paws. Outh'n found it a funny contrast to Oowah's great size.

"Not you, my friend. The villagers would kill you without a thought. They'd think you were there for a feast." Outh'n sighed. "I need to hurry. Mt. Charan's the only place where it might be possible for me to gain a hearing."

The elongated snout dipped and tilted to one side, as if Oowah had trouble understanding.

"I'm going to Mt. Charan. I won't ask you to go with me because this is your home," he waved at the forest surrounding them. "I'm not sure there will be enough prey to hunt. You should stay here."

The muzzle shook back and forth so vigorously, spittle flew. Some landed on Outh'n.

"Ugh! What'd you do that for?"

"Uuff," came the guttural reply, punctuated with one more soft shake of his head, distinctly animal yet understandable.

"Alright, but don't say I didn't warn you. And I've got no more jerked meat to share with you. I can forage when we're out of the forest, but I don't know if a hunt will be successful."

Oowah's only reply was a disdainful shake of his head as he trotted off. Outh'n hoped they were heading in the right direction.

FIVE DAWNINGS BROUGHT the two to the southern edge of the forest. The foothills rose to Outh'n's left and a mountain valley spread out before them. Without trees to block it, the whistling wind nipped Outh'n's cheeks and nose, a harsher warning than Oowah's. Without thinking, he rested one hand on his friend's head and scratched behind his ears.

"It's on the other side of those foothills."

Oowah nodded.

"Think we can get across without being spotted?"

Another nod.

Outh'n snorted. "I know you can, Oowah, but can I?"

The only answer Outh'n received was Oowah's wagging tail disappearing into the tall grasses. He had to jog to catch up. Clusters of hardy wildflowers dotted the area and he couldn't help thinking how much Alanyin would've loved this place. Outh'n returned his gaze to Oowah's tail-tip, which peeked above the grasses. It was all he could see of his friend.

Another three dawnings saw them across the meadow and foothills. Outh'n's stomach burned with worry the entire time, making the otherwise pleasant trek uncomfortable. In the end, they reached the foot of Mt. Charan without meeting a soul.

"Here's where things get tricky," he cautioned Oowah. "There's nowhere to hide on the path, at least for me," he clarified as he grinned over at Oowah. His friend grinned and nodded proudly. "If we meet anyone, you may have to leave me to hide. I don't want your blood on my hands, Iyaba."

Iyaba? Since when had this wuveia become his family? Outh'n shook his head, accepted the feelings lodged in his heart, and continued. "If you stick by me all the way to the top, I think the Guardian will allow you to stay as long as you don't threaten anyone. I'll try to convince him, anyway." Outh'n grimaced, remembering his failures in Prichud. "I haven't done so well before, but I'll do my best. Ailiin tells me I'm better with my hands."

Oowah nudged him forward, poking his snout into Outh'n's lower back. "Alright, alright, I'm going."

The long climb took the better part of a dawning. Min, Dahl, and the leading edge of Shotha, along with a few stars, lit the cloudless sky-dome before Outh'n arrived at the gate. He took just a moment to remember Babeiya's constellation lessons, then looked down. Oowah was still by his side. A good thing he was, too, for twice he almost fell, tripping over small chunks of rock on the trail. Both times, the wuveia rescued him, albeit roughly. The holes in his tunic and skin bore witness to Oowah's loyalty and quick reflexes.

He turned to see how far they'd come and said, "Well, Iyaba, we've arrived."

Oowah nodded once.

"What's this?" The high-pitched, sharp tenor behind them startled both, and Oowah loosed a menacing growl. Had Outh'n not realized the reason, he'd have reacted badly. Quickly, he soothed with hand and voice, "Peace, Iyaba. This is the Guardian." Outh'n bowed.

"Indeed! How is it you know me, tiav'yag? I must confess I don't recognize you."

Outh'n could barely see the little man's features, but his long trailing mustache and beard twitched, catching the dim lights of the sky-dome when he spoke. A grin tugged at Outh'n's lips.

"You find something funny in bringing a wuveia into this holy place?"

"No, Honored Guardian. My apologies." He bowed again for good measure. "My name is Outh'n Durr. I was born in Prichud, a small farming village. My apologies for stepping foot into the holy place without permission. There's an urgent matter and only you can help."

"I hear you clearly, youngling." There was a long pause as the Guardian inspected him and eyed Oowah with distrust. "Is this animal yours, then?"

Outh'n cocked his head to the side. "Not really. He adopted me when all others cast me out."

"He is welcome, then, for we are all Children of Y'Dahnndrya, are we not?" The balding head bobbed once, the stars shining dully upon it. "Follow me, both of you. You cannot stay in the main hall, but there is a place for you."

"That's not really necessary, Honored Guardian," Outh'n hesitated.

"What do you mean?" the little man snapped, his bushy brows slanting sharply as he frowned.

Outh'n's gut clenched. "I meant no offense, Honored Guardian. I need to send a message of warning to my sadau. It's impossible for me to return in person. If you sent a message for me, though, they would certainly get it. No one would dare hinder a message from a Guardian."

"Follow me, Outh'n Durr, tiav'yag. You and your friend need rest because your journey will be long and hard when you leave here." The thin shoulders drooped as he added, "And I fear, more trials await you before you'll learn your purpose."

Outh'n sighed. "I'm used to it, Honored Guardian. It's all I've known. Can't you see my eye? My cheek? And apparently, even my talents weren't enough, not even among my peers. Being an outcast is all I remember, my small family and one friend, now with Tugansol, are the only exceptions." He snorted in disgust. "Sadness you say? A long hard journey, you say? When has my life ever been anything besides that?"

Rather than answer, the little man said, "You may call me Seth Yi'in or Guardian Yi'in if you wish to remain formal. Tugansol's revelation to me gives you the right of the former, though. I doubt we'll meet again in person, so I'm letting you know now." Turning on his heel, he barked, "Come on. The wind bites tonight." He sped through the intricately carved wooden arch.

Outh'n wondered at the man's words but followed as silently as Oowah, who pranced at his side. The Guardian led them to a small outbuilding furnished simply with a grass-stuffed mat, a colorful blanket, a low table holding a small bowl of fruit and nuts, a single bon'jii in his favorite shade of blue, and a pitcher of water. In the far corner, a small shelf held the basic elements — a smoking candle, a vial of water, and a tiny saucer of dirt — reminders of Tugansol's provision for the creation.

"Thank you, Seth Yi'in," Outh'n figured he should test the limits.

"You are most welcome, Outh'n Durr. And whether or not you believe it, Tugansol has guided your footsteps all along your life journey. It's shameful for you to say otherwise." The wooden door snapped shut, and the Guardian was gone before Outh'n could reply.

"He knows nothing of me or my life. How can he say that with such certainty?" Outh'n spoke toward the door as he shook his head. He dropped his pack beside the portal and yanked on the handle to yell, "Guardian Yi'in!" When he turned, Outh'n thought better of his words and amended them. "Oowah can't eat these provisions."

A nod was the only reply he received, but strangely, he knew all would be well. "It's alright, Iyaba. You'll eat well this dusking."

Oowah nodded and padded over to the grass mat to flop down on his side. Outh'n chuckled at the wuveia's obvious satisfaction. At the table, he poured a bowl of water for Oowah and placed it beside him, then filled a goblet for himself. He drained it in a single draught, then poured another and fished around in the bowl. Of the contents, grinja nuts were his favorite. When he collected a handful, he popped them into his mouth all at once. A paryl caught his eye next. The crisp, tart fruit refreshed him and paired well with the nuts.

Finally, he popped the bon'jii into his mouth and chewed slowly, savoring the dessert. Though the flavor started sweet on the soft outer shell, the tart twist at the creamy center didn't disappoint. He sighed in satisfaction. The last time he'd had bon'jiis was when he won his last target shooting competition. He'd been twelve and Alanyin had been cheering for him alongside his family. Anger stirred the smoldering coals within him, souring the memory.

The door of their lodging burst open as an attendant brought in a platter containing a pile of meat. Outh'n watched closely as the man placed it at Oowah's head. A little taller than Seth Yi'in, the man retreated as quickly as he'd come. Outh'n didn't even have the chance to thank him.

"Maybe we should keep watch tonight, Oowah," he murmured to the wuveia who had wasted no time clearing the platter. Outh'n's eyes never left the door.

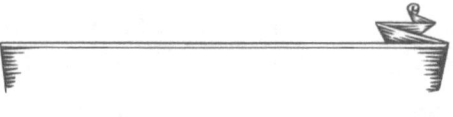

8 Explanations

The light of dawning shot through a window set close to the ceiling. Brilliant glashiin panes patterned the floor in a colorful array thanks to the rising suns. Outh'n moved the table and climbed up to inspect the etching. That's how Seth Yi'in's attendant found him.

"Visitor," he ground out the greeting, clearly upset. "You need to come with me. The Guardian calls and he is a busy man. You can leave your beast here." The man jabbed a thick finger tipped with a pristine nail at Oowah, whose whisper soft growl-snuff was just loud enough the attendant flinched.

"My friend will go with me. If he isn't welcome inside, then I'll wait here." Outh'n's words, though quiet, rang with unshakable obstinacy.

"What's taking so long, Mikail?" Seth Yi'in's high tenor wavered through the open portal.

"My apologies, Honored Guardian," Mikail's chin dipped once as he continued. "This wandering tiav'yag," he sneered and slitted his eyes at Outh'n, "refuses to leave the beast here."

Seth Yi'in frowned, first at the attendant, then at Outh'n, who'd chosen to perch against the edge of the table. Stretching his legs out, he placed one booted foot atop the other at the ankles. Folded arms across his chest added to the picture of confidence he hoped he could pull off. For several moments, he watched the interaction between the two men in silence. A grin tugged one corner of his lips up.

"Outh'n Durr is our guest, Mikail, and you will treat him appropriately. His friend is also a guest. What kind of insanity has overtaken you that you'd rile a wuveia?" The Guardian threw up his hands in disgust and shook his head hard enough to set his wispy beard dancing.

Outh'n's jaw dropped in surprise. When he realized, he snapped it shut so hard his teeth rattled. He replaced his shock with a determined scowl.

Seth Yi'in's eyes missed nothing. "Outh'n Durr, are you playing us for fools?"

He shook his head as he answered honestly, "Not at all, Honored Guardian."

"Then what's going on?"

Outh'n gestured toward Mikail. "He said Oowah couldn't go with me. I said if that was the case, I'd wait here. This place is strange to him and I don't want to leave him among unfamiliar people."

Seth Yi'in nodded. "Of course. I'm sorry for the difficulties. Oowah," he cut a piercing glance toward the wuveia who'd risen to stand beside Outh'n, "may join us." He nodded politely to Oowah. How much of the Guardian's actions were for show? Outh'n wondered whether he'd been wise to come here. But wise or not, Ailiin's life and chance of happiness hung in the balance. Saving her would always be worth any risk to himself.

"Lead the way, Guardian Yi'in," Outh'n gestured with one hand and placed the other on Oowah's neck.

They entered the main temple door and followed the central hallway for quite some time, turning neither left nor right. At the end of the hall, a door nestled in the wall on Outh'n's right. Seth Yi'in led them into the small room which housed a square table set with writing materials, three shelves filled to overflowing with scrolls, and two upholstered chairs with armrests. A small brazier crackled in the far corner. Smoke exited through a hole in the ceiling.

"This is my private study," Seth Yi'in informed them. "You may leave us, Mikail."

"As you say, Honored Guardian." The odious attendant left, closing the door quietly behind him.

"Now, Outh'n Durr," he began as he settled into one chair, "what's so important about this message? What's your trouble?"

"I don't mean trouble for me, Honored Guardian," he answered quietly. He waved a hand toward the opposite chair and his eyebrow rose in question.

"Yes, yes. Sit!" The Guardian nodded and gestured impatiently.

"I see you wish us to be on our way as quickly as possible." Outh'n sighed with resignation. After all, what did he expect? "I was hiding in the bushes at the side of an animal track when I overheard a conversation between two of my old acquaintances from home. Apparently, they were hunting me." Outh'n frowned and turned his lazy eye away from the Guardian.

"Have no fear, Outh'n. I will listen and judge as well as I can." The tinny voice might be sharp, but his eyes focused on Outh'n didn't waver. His sincerity was easy to see.

Outh'n nodded and continued. "When they found some items I'd lost from my pack when I fled, they assumed the wuveia pack had gotten to me first. One of them threatened to wed my unsuspecting sadau, vowing she would suffer in my place." He shook his head in disgust. "I couldn't let it go, but I wasn't able to do anything, either. I'm already under sentence. And if I failed, my death wouldn't keep him from hurting my family."

Seth Yi'in steepled his fingers and rested his nose on the peak. "I see," he murmured. "You did well coming here instead. How many dawnings?"

"Too many," mumbled Outh'n, swiping a hand over his mouth and chin, feeling the growth of beard there. "At least five dawnings since I saw them. I could be mistaken. The dawnings run together when you have nothing to mark the difference between them." He paused and ran a hand through his unruly brown hair. "I believe close to three nainda have passed in all since they forced me from my home without cause."

The Guardian's eyes snapped to his, flashing fire. "You dare to speak against your village council, youngling?"

"Only because it's the truth," he shook his head sadly. "My village has hated me for many tsimikin." He laid his head against the back of his chair. "But I'm no murderer. And even if I was, what murderer kills a friend? The only person besides family who took the time to get to know them?" Outh'n stood, unable to keep still. The room was small, especially with Oowah sprawled on the floor by the door, but Outh'n paced, anyway.

"I know this probably sounds crazy to you, but I give you my word of honor." He snorted, realizing that probably meant little with the brand still healing on his cheek. "I mean it. You have my word of honor, despite this," he gestured roughly to his cheek, having to turn his crooked eye toward the Guardian, "that I did not murder my best friend." He dropped back into the chair, propped his elbows on his knees, and cupped his face in his hands. "I loved her, wanted to ask her to be my life-mate. How could I do that if she was dead?"

Tears burned his eyes, and he allowed them to fall. Oowah's claws scraped and ticked on the smooth stone floor as he came closer. The great, shaggy head butted him as his friend offered the only comfort available to him. Outh'n fell to his knees on the floor and hugged the furry neck. Oowah patiently waited, crooning and snuffing now and again.

A creak alerted him to the Guardian moving and he jumped. "Now, now," Seth Yi'in soothed as he scratched away with stiil on partra, "Enough of that. I believe you, Outh'n Durr. There are dark things moving under the surface of what we see with our eyes. Your case isn't isolated, I'm afraid. While I can't undo the sentence, I can send the message for you. I hope it will reach your family in time."

"Thank you, Honored Guardian," Outh'n whispered in awe. Someone besides the beast at his side believed him. Tugansol had not abandoned him.

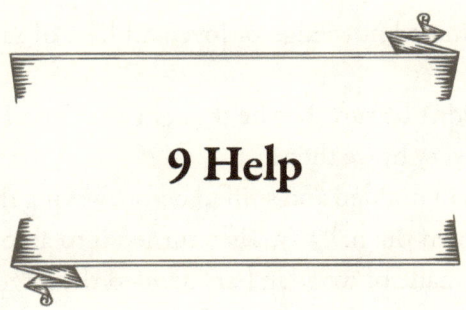

9 Help

The stiil scratched longer than Outh'n would've thought necessary. When he couldn't stand it anymore, the question inside him exploded far more grouchy than he'd planned. "How long does it take to jot down a simple warning?"

Seth Yi'in barked a laugh. "Little you know, youngling. One must choose the correct words for such a missive to be believed. As a Guardian, I can't lie or it compromises my effectiveness and hinders my relationship with our blessed Creator." He rolled the small piece of partra and sealed it with sepi, the seal of Mt. Charan Shrine sinking in deep. "Follow me, please," he urged as he rose and opened the door.

They walked back down the hall. Upon reaching the entry room, Outh'n noticed intricate mosaics decorating the upper portion of the walls. "The glashiin work and mosaics are beautiful here."

"Mhmm." Seth Yi'in headed for a doorway on the left. This hallway rose two steps higher, but the panoramic artisan work continued.

So the Guardian didn't want to talk about them? Outh'n kept silent, but studied the subject of each section as much as he could. Something strange caught his eye, though, and he found his tongue had other ideas.

"That one there," he pointed up and to the left, "what's in the tree's branches?"

"Not a tree, or a 'that', Outh'n Durr." Seth Yi'in paused his quick march to explain. "She is Edrea, one of the Terreilia of old. She sacrificed much during the Great Cataclysm. Of all who lived, perhaps she gained the most knowledge of love and loss, of sacrificing self for the good of all others."

Outh'n couldn't be sure, but he thought the Guardian's eyes turned glassy. "She was very brave then?"

The small man nodded and sniffed before waving them to follow as he continued down the hallway. They turned into an open archway on the left. A door made of wooden bars divided the large room into two sections, the inner much larger than the outer.

"Kyna? Loryn? Are you here?" The scuff of hide boots on stone heralded the arrival of a burly woman with shoulders wider than Kurg'l's stepped through the barred door.

"What can I do for you, Guardian Yi'in?"

"I have a message for the Durr family at Prichud Village. It must arrive in three dawnings, Loryn. Can I count on you?"

The woman glared at Outh'n's brand and a scowl marred her smooth, broad brow. "For this miscreant, Honored Guardian? Why?" Her soft, almost hypnotic voice became an acidic hiss as she spoke of Outh'n.

He couldn't help it. He rolled his eyes. And received a backhand in his stomach. Not hateful, but just enough to remind him Seth Yi'in was the only reason he remained safe inside the temple walls. He sighed and bowed his head, mumbling an apology to the Guardian.

"This man is a tiav'yag, yes, but he is also my guest, Loryn. You will show him the proper courtesy." The words, though soft, tumbled hard as obsyn stone.

"Yes, Honored Guardian. My apologies, Guest." Outh'n let go of the hissed word, 'guest.' Her attitude was expected. Besides that, her opinion mattered little as long as the message got to Ailiin.

"Now then, Loryn, who is your fastest rider?"

"Meren, but he's out." Short, clipped tones conveyed her displeasure.

"Didn't I just see him in the outer hall?"

"Perhaps you did, Honored Guardian. If so, he hasn't checked in with me yet." She turned back toward the larger section and loosed a whistle that rang in Outh'n's ears and set Oowah to whining.

"A wuveia?" Loryn shrieked in horror. "Honored Guardian, why would you allow that creature in here?"

"He will not harm any creature within these walls." Outh'n couldn't be certain, but he thought the Guardian's grinding jaw meant he was losing patience.

"But they are natural enemies, they and the arb'la," Loryn sputtered.

"I will not tell you again, Loryn. This man is our guest. His friend is also our guest. They know there are rules here and neither has given me any reason to doubt they will follow them."

"Yes, Honored Guardian," Loryn's voice was subdued and respectful, but her middawn, sky-dome blue eyes promised swift retribution if her arb'la suffered. Arb'la were the swiftest of the domesticated cattle in Shinnoah. Outh'n felt sure his missive would arrive in time.

"Loryn, you called for me?" The willowy young maid that stepped through the barred door next had a voice like rain bells. Her eyes were the same blue as Loryn's, but her hair was a much lighter shade of brown. Rather than having it cut short at the shoulders like the broader woman, she'd let hers grow long and had plaited it over one shoulder. The end reached her hip.

"Kyna, go to the entry hall and find Meren. Send him to us, please." Loryn's command brooked no rebellion.

"Yes, Sadau." The girl glanced at Outh'n, appreciative at first. Confusion wrinkled her brow when she spotted his brand. Then she paled when she saw Oowah. She edged carefully past Outh'n. Her worried gaze settled on Oowah, who had no intention of moving. She crept past him on tiptoe, narrowly missing his snout-tip, and scurried out the door without looking back.

In no time, she returned with a short, wiry lad bearing a shock of white-blond hair. Dirt smudged one cheek and a streak of red arched over the other. Blood?

"What happened to you, young Meren?" Seth Yi'in asked in that clipped way he used when Outh'n had first arrived.

"Ah, a prickly branch snuck past my guard, kissing my hand and caressing my lovely face, Honored Guardian," he joked. "It's nothing a bit of Lus' salve won't cure," he shrugged it off.

"Despite that, how quickly could you be ready to ride again?" Seth Yi'in was taking no chances that Loryn or Kyna would interfere with the instructions. Outh'n breathed deeply in relief and reached out a hand to scratch between Oowah's ears and behind them.

"Eiya! You've got a wuveia, Honored Guest?" There was no mistaking the gleam of admiration in the lad's eyes. Outh'n smiled in return, waiting for the moment Meren spotted his cheek.

"I don't. He's a friend who chose to stay with me. Oowah's free to come and go. I would never cage a beast of the wilds."

"May I touch him?"

Outh'n looked first to Loryn, whose eyebrows rose in dismay, though she clamped her lips together. Kyna paled and Seth Yi'in simply nodded his own ascent. "Well, I don't know. Just hold out your hand and see if he's alright with you touching him." Outh'n trembled inside as Oowah took a tentative sniff, snorted, and nodded. "Go ahead. He particularly enjoys a good scratch behind his ears."

Outh'n stepped aside so Meren could proceed. Oowah crooned at the youngling in pleasure and butted him when he stopped. Meren laughed. When he looked at Outh'n again, he spotted the brand. The happiness in his eyes dimmed, but instead of censure, sadness replaced it. He gestured to the wound. "What happened?"

Not 'what did you do' or 'why should I help you' but 'what happened?' A sound he'd never made before wobbled in his throat. He cleared it before answering. "They said I killed the woman I loved with all my heart."

"Your life-mate?"

Outh'n shook his head. "I never got to ask her," he answered in a hoarse half-whisper as his eyes burned with tears he couldn't shed here. "She slipped on a tree branch and fell from too high up. I couldn't get to her in time to catch her. She was dead before I even got to her side. I couldn't even bid her farewell." His brow furrowed, and he turned his face to look up at the skylights high above.

A sudden touch at his sleeve startled him. Meren jerked away. "I meant no harm, Honored Guest," he soothed. "I just wanted to say I was sorry."

"My name is Outh'n, if you care to utter it." Outh'n took a risk offering his name. He shrugged and turned his branded cheek away.

"Outh'n, I'm Meren and pleased to meet anyone who's friends with a wuveia." Meren smiled broadly.

"So where's this message, Guardian Seth?" Meren turned to the thinner man, an eyebrow raised in query.

"Here," he snapped as he lifted the missive. "But I forbid you to leave if you haven't rested since your last ride. This message is too important. You can't fail. Come," he motioned to Outh'n and Meren. "Outh'n and I will walk with you to see Lus and get your face taken care of."

"And I can tell you how the last ride went," Meren added.

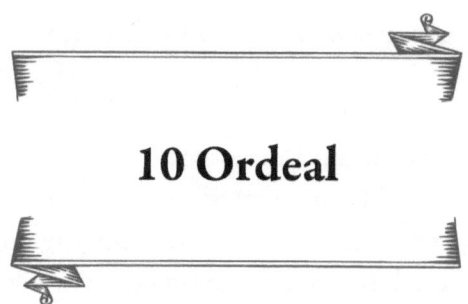

10 Ordeal

A dimly lit, wood paneled room confused Outh'n when he woke. The scent of smoldering wood sent pangs of homesickness radiating through his muscles. Trying to stretch was a mistake. Outh'n groaned when he realized the pain seizing his muscles wasn't a result of missing his family. He nestled deeper into the lush mattress beneath him, seeking relief.

With his eyes clamped shut, memories overwhelmed him. The last thing he remembered was riding on a canyon path with the wind shrieking relentlessly in his ears. Meren, who'd proven to be a genuine friend, left before Outh'n had finished gathering his things to leave.

"What's wrong with the people of Prichud, Outh'n?" Meren had asked before mounting his arb'la. "I've only known you for a few hesps, but I'll never understand how they could believe you'd kill someone." With a shake of his head, he promised to make sure the missive reached his family in two nainda.

Outh'n scoffed, sorrow burning his eyes. "Believe it, Meren. There are people who are less civilized than the beasts of the wilds." Meren chuckled and Outh'n just stared at him until his mirth died. "Believe it, friend. I have lived it every day of my life. This eye." He stopped and shook his head. "No, I thought this eye was the reason the others left me out of everything and the maidens stayed away. I guess I was wrong because I heard one say it was my ability to win competitions." He checked his pack over again as he continued. "Add to that I had an apprenticeship lined up with expert glashiin workers down Oxyl way."

"Jealousy? That bad?" Outh'n glanced up at him, grinning when he saw Meren's hand scratching away at Oowah's ears. The latter's tongue lolled happily.

His grin faded as he answered. "I wouldn't have thought so. Not until I heard it from Kurg'l's own mouth. I didn't exactly live a glorious life. My babeiya and moyri worked a farm, a poor one at that. I had no friends until Alanyin pushed her way into my life. My family was, still is, everything to me." A knot built in his throat and choked off anything else he might've said.

"Well, my friend, I hope it's alright for me to call you that." Meren waited for Outh'n's nod before he said, "I'm off to deliver this." He held up the rolled missive. "Pray for my success."

"I will Meren, though I'm not sure how often Tugansol hears me."

"You doubt the very Breath of Life?" The surprise on Meren's face had Outh'n chuckling wryly.

"If you'd lived my life, you'd understand what I mean. I believe in Tugansol. I'm even starting to believe there's some kind of purpose for my existence." Outh'n looked around for Oowah, who loped over to him while licking his lips. He stood patiently at Outh'n's right side. "Who besides Tugansol would send me a wuveia friend and a faithful messenger, or who would bend the ears of a Guardian to my plea? The Giver of Life is the only answer I can come up with." He shrugged. "I will pray. That's all I can promise you, Meren."

"And I will promise you one more thing, Outh'n Durr. I will send your family your well wishes."

Outh'n shook his head immediately. "Please don't, Meren. If they know I live, the ones who came after me before would stop at nothing, it seems, to see me dead."

"Are you a coward, then?" Meren's eyes twinkled with mischief a moment before he shuttered them.

Outh'n stared in silence before deciding the question wasn't a jibe. "No. But I'd hate to know they'd harm my family if they can't find me.

I'm making certain neither they nor anyone else will find me when I leave here today."

"But," Meren began, but Outh'n cut him off.

"You must go, my friend. I thank you for your short friendship with me, for your promise, and your concern for my family and me. There's no safe place for me in Shinnoah. Oowah, the Guardian, and you are the only people I've met since my sentencing who treated me with courtesy. Well," he checked himself, "there's also Bazhbet Mehya." He shrugged. "I'm going far away. With Tugansol's guidance, may I never put a foot wrong on the path."

Meren nodded slowly and smiled. A cheerful wave preceded a cloud of dust as he urged the graceful mount into a gallop and disappeared. Outh'n watched him until he disappeared around a bend in the path, then set off at a quick pace after him. The shrill voice of the Guardian halted him.

"Wait, Outh'n Durr! You younglings are always in such a hurry," he grumbled. "I have a mount for you. You do ride, do you not?" He smirked, raised his eyebrows, and cocked his head.

"Of course I ride, Honored Guardian," Outh'n smirked back. "I didn't get many chances to ride arb'la back home. But Babeiya taught me well on our d'kine."

"Then here. This is Eilse. She will carry you faithfully and speed you on your way. Go to Chefvna, to Bazhbet Mehya, the Senya there."

Outh'n stiffened. "I know him."

Seth Yi'in blinked in surprise. "How?"

"He came to my trial and spoke for me and my family. He's the reason I'm standing here instead of swinging from a tree limb."

The Guardian nodded. "Then you know he's a good man. Find him. Ask him for a boat. Then make the crossing to Yacan. It's the safest place for you."

It was Outh'n's turn to gape in surprise. "The Forbidden place? Safer there? How?"

"Don't worry about that. Just keep heading north. No matter what happens, keep heading north to Chefvna. Bazhbet will help you from there. I've included a map in the arb'la's pack."

Outh'n nodded, struck dumb by this news. In all his life, he would never have thought the island where so many died would actually be a haven for anyone. He mounted Eilse and clicked at her, lightly kicking with his heels as he'd learned.

"Thank you, Honored Guardian. I will pray blessings over you when I next offer them up."

A HIDDEN DOOR CREAKED open and shattered Outh'n's concentration. He bolted upright. Or tried to. In the end, it was a losing battle with the mattress and blankets surrounding him. Not only that, he ached everywhere.

"Calm down, Outh'n Durr. It's only me, Bazhbet Mehya." The gruff stage-whisper warned Outh'n others might be listening.

Outh'n's heart raced. He breathed deep, measuring each to slow down his racing heart. "Where am I? What is this place?"

"It's a safe room. Many have needed to come here. I'm sure there will be many more. But the village itself isn't safe for you. We must be careful."

"Where's Oowah? And Eilse?" Dread forced its way into his stomach, worry looming large for his friends and traveling companions.

"I haven't seen anyone." Bazhbet looked at him askance, as if he suddenly wasn't sure of Outh'n's state of mind.

"Oowah is my friend, a wuveia, and Eilse is my mount, an arb'la."

Bazhbet's face fell. "A wuveia and an arb'la, you say?"

Outh'n nodded as nausea started an unpleasant dance in his stomach. Bazhbet's brows drew down in anger. Outh'n paled as the man rose to his full height and puffed up his chest.

"You leave tonight, Outh'n Durr." The clipped words left Outh'n wondering what he'd done to raise the Senya's ire. "Your pack is there," he waved to the left, "in that corner. Make sure you have all you need or think you'll need. I'll be back after the suns have truly set. Be ready." And he slipped out the door as silently as he'd entered.

What had happened to his companions? What had happened to him? How had he gotten here? And how would he win Bazhbet back to his side?

Swinging his legs out from under the blankets slowly achieved greater results than his previous panicked struggle to get out of bed. He padded over to his pack, soreness strangling every muscle and searing each joint. His ribs and face were on fire. He looked around, but there was no mirror in the room. Tentative fingers traced over the planes of his face, hissing as he identified a couple of extremely sore spots, one near his good eye, the other closer to his chin. He tried removing his tunic, grunting in pain when he lifted his arms to pull the collar up and over his head. Looking down, his chest was more purple than the usual golden tan and the curling hair sprinkled across it did little to hide the damage. Someone had secured a small square patch to his left side, where a sharp pain met his inquiring touch. He winced and groaned again as he struggled with his pack. He'd have to loosen up before tonight because leaving wouldn't be a leisurely stroll.

He checked the contents as instructed and found he had more than enough. He rose and stretched a little until the pain almost knocked him out. Once he caught his breath again, he explored the confines of his room. He'd made a note of the secret door and kept away from that wall. The wall on the right hid a refreshing room and a small storage space hid behind the left wall. After visiting the refreshing room, he felt more like himself, determined to face whatever bad news was surely coming.

Oowah would be here with him if he lived. He didn't want to think of it, but couldn't help himself. A small stack of kindling sat in one corner and he reached into it. Fishing out the biggest piece, he held it in both hands and snapped it in two. It wasn't enough. He fished out another. He'd worked his way through most of the basket when Bazhbet returned.

"What are you doing, Outh'n Durr? Come on!"

Outh'n hurried to his discarded shirt, slipped it on, carefully slipping his pack onto his left shoulder, away from his injured side, and stepped through the wooden portal behind Bazhbet.

11 Crossing

Angry voices echoed in the distance as the two men sped away. Bazhbet had exited first, then beckoned Outh'n to follow. He stayed as close as he dared, keeping watch on the Senya and his own footing. He couldn't afford another injury.

Waves rushing at the shore warned Outh'n the sea was nearby. The murmur grew to a rhythmic thundering, which he would've found pleasant in other circumstances, as a wood and stone pier emerged out of the darkness. A small skiiv with a single sail bobbed crazily in the swell as a shadowy figure moved busily from one end of the vessel to the other.

"I'm sorry, Outh'n," Bazhbet spoke only loud enough to be heard over the noise. "This was the best I could do. He was the only one I could trust to get you to safety. Keep an eye on the sky. The end of Y'ma isn't the best time for sailing. When you get to Yacan, touch nothing but the roots at the shore. Wait there until she comes for you, no matter how long it takes. Only that person can lead you safely on."

"She?" The puzzle didn't take long to figure out. The Senya had to mean Serafin, the Guardian of Yacan.

Bazhbet gripped one of Outh'n's shoulders gently as a babeiya might say goodbye to his abei. "I will pray for your safety. Honor Tugansol always, youngling. Never forget your valiant friends who gave their lives to protect you. They kept you safe until I arrived. Eilse is recovering, but Oowah, they shot. The feathered ends of six arrows told a grim tale as they pointed the way to his body. I buried him and will remember him with you."

Tears streamed down Outh'n's face at the news he had known was coming, but hoped he wouldn't have to hear.

"Go now! Now!" Bazhbet shoved him toward the small sailing vessel. He didn't stay to watch them leave and hurried back inland.

"Come now, Master Durr," a nasally baritone voice urged from the pier. "We must set sail now or lose the help o' the tide."

Outh'n forced his feet toward the skiiv. Woodenly, he hauled his pack over the side and followed it awkwardly.

"Know ye anythin' of sailing?"

"No, Senya," answered Outh'n in a blank monotone, which masked his breaking heart.

"Then you'll need to learn. I'll need help if we're to get you there safely."

"But how will you return, Senya?"

A wry chuckle broke over the swishing waves. "Smart mouth on ye, then! No master are you! The Senya gave you more credit than was due you, methinks."

Outh'n rose to his feet. He wasn't as tall as Kurg'l, but he could carry himself well. "What do you need me to do, Senya?" Exhaustion and despair bled out of him. He could hear it in his own voice, no matter how he wanted to show his competence.

"Nah. Sit ye down back where ye were. I'll have us out on the open sea in no time. I'll let ye know when I need a pair of younger arms and legs." The older man nodded and pointed toward Outh'n's pack. Outh'n nodded back and settled beside it.

They sailed all dusking and well into the next dawning when the puffy clouds which had greeted them at first light grew ominous.

"Looks like we can't avoid it, youngling," yelled the sailor over the rising wind. "I'm definitely gonna need your help and ye'll need to listen carefully. Do only and exactly what I tell ye to. One slip and we'll be sleeping with the jimla in the deeps."

"Yes, Senya," Outh'n answered as he rose stiffly and stretched.

Even with Outh'n's help, things were difficult. Though fighting seasickness, he was determined to help the old man get him to the shores of Yacan. He wasn't sure why. Death was almost as certain in one place as in the other. Still, the old man didn't deserve to die because of his indifference.

"We're almost through!" The sailor worked hard to be heard over the howl of the wind. "See the golden line over there?"

Outh'n blinked away the rain on his lashes without letting up on the rope in his hands. He yelled back, "Yes!"

And that was his mistake. He shouldn't have tried to speak. Vomit soon covered the decking nearest him, his clothes, and boots. Ignoring it all, he clung to the rope and to the hope his legs wouldn't prove as weak as his belly. When he no longer felt the grip of nausea, he raised his head and rose from his knees, adjusting his grip on the rope.

"Well, look at ye! A true sailor, ye are, Master Durr." With the wind dying down, Outh'n could hear the admiration in the old man's tone. Encouraged, he nodded his thanks, careful to keep his mouth closed this time.

The old man chuckled. "Well, look where we are." His bony finger pointed toward the bow. "There be Yacan, straight ahead."

Outh'n turned to see a misty shape hovering in the distance, half hidden by the curtain of rain which was speeding away from them. He fell to his knees again.

"Don't give up now, youngling. There's still a ways to go." The old man helped him to his feet and walked him over to his pack. He gently inspected Outh'n's red, raw hands. He whistled. "Ye are a determined one, ain't ye? Why didn't ye let go?"

Outh'n looked into the old man's eyes and raised one eyebrow. "I hear jimla kick in their sleep."

The old man cackled in glee and patted him roughly on the shoulder. Outh'n offered a tired smile in return.

"See if you can sleep a bit and I'll get us as close as I can to the shore. You may have to swim, though. Think you can with that heavy pack?"

"I'll leave my pack if I have to swim. On Yacan, if I live, Serafin will make sure I don't die. If I die, what need would I have for a pack of supplies?"

The old man nodded. "So it is."

Moment by moment, the island loomed nearer. The shadows gave way to some definition. He rested, but he couldn't sleep. Leaves and branches dominated the view. A thud on the bottom of the skiiv sent a shudder through Outh'n.

"Well, looks like we're here."

Outh'n nodded and stood. Seeing the roots were near, he shouldered his pack and prepared to trade the known for the unknown.

"I'm sure the Senya told you not to touch anything, to wait for her to guide you safely in?"

"He did."

"Follow those directions and you'll be fine. Everyone gets exactly what they deserve on Yacan."

Outh'n stared at the older man for a long time before he nodded and stepped off onto a nearby root. He nearly slipped but made it to a circle of roots, which seemed to have a solid enough bottom. He set his pack there and settled down to wait.

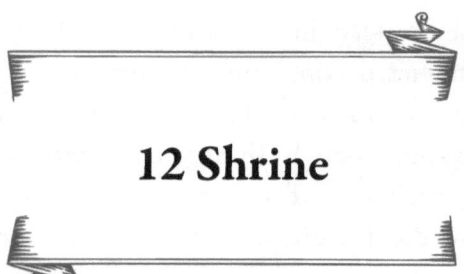

12 Shrine

What was taking Serafin so long? Two dawnings passed with no other sounds except the waves lapping at the roots and a gentle rustle of leaves above and around him. Too long. Too quiet.

Being left alone with his thoughts wasn't exactly how he thought he'd spend the last dawnings of his life. His people had stripped him of every joy he'd known. Shaking his head at the unfairness, he wished he could go back and throw a couple of tournaments. If that's all it would've taken, he'd have done it in a heartbeat. But was it even possible they'd have accepted him if he'd been handsome and compliant as a bizhal?

His head dropped into his hands. Outh'n groaned and ruffled his hair, which was becoming shaggy. The growth of beard probably wasn't the neatest or cleanest either. When he arrived, he'd quickly rinsed his sick-soiled clothing, but he hadn't really cleansed himself.

The suns were setting again, but there was still time. He stripped off his vest, tunic, and breeches. The woolen socks Moyri had knitted as a birthing day gift followed, setting off a pang of homesickness. He left his undergarments on. Who knew when Serafin would arrive? She might wait until his guard was down. Keeping his eyes open, he washed as well as he could with a small bar of soap and a rough scrap of cloth. He saved his hair and face for last, knowing he'd be most vulnerable then. He donned fresh garments from his pack before dunking his head quickly, several times, breaking in between each, to make certain he was still alone. A quick lathering of soap in his hair probably wasn't the greatest wash he'd ever done, but it would have to do. He repeated the dunking process. Then it was time for his face. He scrubbed it and lathered up his beard, then splashed his face, keeping careful watch between each rinse.

Outh'n felt the shift in the atmosphere immediately. Someone was near. He didn't know how he knew, but he did. The only piece of garb left was the clean vest. He shrugged it on, not bothering to dry his face and hair completely. Shaking away the excess moisture, he scanned the shadows. His crooked eye would have thrown him off tsimikin ago, but he'd learned to ignore distractions.

Another intense scan revealed a shadow unlike its surroundings. Not exactly human, but certainly not a plant.

"Who's there?" Outh'n's voice shook, and he chided himself. How could a coward prove his worth to a warrior Guardian?

The shadow moved, straightened, and grew larger, though not by much, as it stalked closer. If this was Serafin, she was but a youngling, younger than himself, though he knew height wasn't always a reliable sign of age. One of his relatives had seen ten more tsimikin than he and was a full head and shoulders shorter. It was best to err on the side of caution.

Should he call out again? Outh'n opted to hold his tongue. The person moved toward him. If his shout wasn't loud enough, there was no reason for Serafin to come closer. Patience seemed to have a great value here, and he was certain caution was best, so he quieted the clamor in his mind. Whatever was coming, whoever was, he wanted to be ready.

"You can relax, Outh'n Durr." Though her voice sounded youthful, it resonated with firm resolve and a confidence which only came with many tsimikin of experience. "I mean you no harm." There was a definite pause before she added, "Yet."

When she stepped into the dim light which remained of the dawning, a slight, wiry figure, still in the formative stage, captivated his attention. From her sun-streaked blond hair cropped short and spiking in all directions, to the short hide boots which covered her dainty feet, she hardly looked like Guardian material. Her eyes were almond-shaped and the most brilliant blue-green, the same color as the leaves above them. Clothing resembling leaves and roots scattered on the ground made it difficult to keep her figure apart from the surrounding area, even as she took a step closer. If she was to lie down, she'd likely disappear. Dirt and clay smudged her pale skin, the darker clay around her eyes making them shine even more brilliantly.

"Serafin?" The squeak which came out of him was nothing close to what Outh'n was aiming for. Heat rushed into his cheeks and ears.

She nodded.

He waited a moment and said in his normal voice, "Ah, you already know I'm Outh'n Durr. I'm not sure what I'm supposed to do here. Bazhbet Mehya sent me."

She nodded again. "Bazhbet is a firm ally and a good Child."

Outh'n cocked his head to one side in wonder. How did this youngling dare to call a Senya a child? "What do you mean, Serafin? He's at least three times my age. Hardly a child."

"We are all Children, or had you forgotten?" Her voice held the sharp tang of a disappointed parent.

He searched his memories, sifting through dusking stories of a time long gone. "Ah, yes. Children of Y'Dahnndrya. I haven't heard the phrase in a very long time."

"More is the pity for your people, Outh'n Durr."

"Just Outh'n is fine, Honored Serafin," he hurried to urge her.

"Just Serafin is fine, Outh'n, as you were calling me before. I am no more honored than you. This place has a hierarchy. This is the truth. But we are all Children." When his brow wrinkled, she added, "You will learn. Follow me."

He made to lift his pack. "Leave it. It will slow you down."

"But," he started and stopped at her raised hand.

"You need not fear for your things here. No one will take them. Leave the pack and place your trust in me."

He stared into her eyes and slowly nodded, though it was probably the hardest thing he'd ever had to do. Climbing out of the nest of roots wasn't easy. They'd become slick, and he had to grip them so hard he broke several of his already short nails and cracked another down the middle. He hissed in pain, but it was nothing compared to the thorns of grief lodged in his heart.

At the rim of the nest, he saw Serafin several steps away and carefully joined her.

"Step where I step and nowhere else, Outh'n, if you wish to live." She turned and her warning continued. "Stay close. I can't guarantee your safety if you don't."

Without another word, she sprang forward. Outh'n was hard-pressed to keep up. And the longer they sprinted, jumping from slippery root to swinging vine, the harder he found it to breathe. Even the air seemed to fight him.

After what seemed a lifetime, a glint of gold flashed through the trees. How it shone was a mystery to him, for the suns were almost set.

Taking his eyes off Serafin was a mistake. He slipped and would've fallen to his death if it wasn't for her quick reflexes. Her grip tightened on his arm and she twisted the tail of his tunic in her other hand. Pulling him back onto the path, she chided, "What did I tell you, Outh'n Durr?"

He nodded, saving his breath for the rest of the journey, as he marveled at the strength in the tiny woman. He knew that would leave a bruise by morrowdawning. The glint of gold grew larger, confirming his suspicion that they were heading to it. When they reached it, Outh'n spied a small, round construction built upon a wooden platform surrounded by trunk-like supports, capped with a leaf-engraved, rounded roof. A central trunk supported this roof in the middle and at the far end, a pair of saplings guarded the opening to what looked like a hallway.

"Rest here for a moment." The warmth of Serafin's tone surprised Outh'n.

She didn't have to tell him twice. He collapsed on the floor palms down, cheek touching the cool, smooth wood, and simply focused on breathing.

"You will need less." Serafin gestured from his head to his boots.

"What do you mean?" he gasped.

"When you catch your breath, rise. I will take you to prepare." The coolness returned to Serafin's voice and left no room for argument.

"Prepare for what?" Words came easier now.

"Save your breath for questions that matter, Outh'n." She chided him.

He nodded, amazed. She treated him as an equal, like he was worth something. Serafin didn't slow down for him because of his eye, didn't shrink away at the mark on his cheek, which remained hairless.

"Are you ready?"

Outh'n nodded. What else could he do? Breathing was still difficult, but his heartbeat had slowed. Sweat streamed down his face, neck, and back. He rose stiffly and followed the woman. She was graceful and conservative in her movements, a lethal deception, he was certain. In comparison, he felt awkward.

Serafin led him between the two trees. They continued down the tree-lined hallway until she stopped in front of a door draped with a vine curtain. Sweeping it aside, she stepped through and beckoned him to follow. A black shadow taller and broader than even Bazhbet Mehya stood at attention against the back wall.

Serafin waved toward him as Outh'n froze. "This is Kol Udota. He will help you prepare."

With those words, she stepped out, leaving him alone with the guard. Upon closer inspection, Outh'n realized his suspicions were true. Kol was Genzetti.

It took a moment to gain the courage, but he finally said, "Greetings, Kol Udota. My name is Outh'n Durr."

"I know," he rumbled in a voice like deep thunder on the mountains. "There's no time to talk. In the chest," he gestured with a huge hand, pointing his thumb toward a wooden box on his right. The metal hinges and clasp were the only decorations on its otherwise smooth surface. "You'll find clothing inside. And over there," he waved toward the opposite corner, "you can refresh yourself. Whatever you need, you'll find it's provided." He moved toward the vine curtain and said, "I'll be outside the door if you have questions about the fit." And with that, he disappeared, as silent as Bazhbet had moved through the secret door.

13 Preparation

Outh'n shook his head and had stepped up to the small table Kol pointed to when the realization struck. There were others on Yacan. Serafin was supposedly alone here, as far as anyone knew. But Kol's presence proved otherwise. What other surprises hid under the cover of Yacan's blue-green leaves and the shadows of its twisted trunks?

Then again, maybe it was just the two of them. Just because no one wanted him wasn't a reason to assume Serafin was in the same position. Kol could be her mate and, if that was so, who was he to judge her choice, strange though it was? But if that was true, then why would Bazhbet send him here?

Pushing the questions aside, Outh'n hurried to clean up. A flat blade lay on the table, so he took a few more moments to shave off his beard, which was indeed scraggly. He also didn't like the itchiness of it. Having freed his face from its hairy prison, he trimmed his hair at the back of his neck and around his ears, shaving the lower edges close to the skin but not all the way to his scalp. When he was done, a shaggy mop of wavy brown just brushed the tips of his ears and eyebrows. He brushed it back and to the left, using his fingers.

Satisfied with his efforts, Outh'n turned to the trunk. Rummaging through the contents, he discovered a pair of new-leaf-green, wide-legged breeches. The legs tapered below the knee and, sewn at a steep angle, was a thick cuff. A thin length of golden fabric, which he took to be a belt, and another thin length of fabric in the same brilliant blue-green as Serafin's eyes were all that remained in the chest. So he had breeches and his choice of a belt. He chose the gold and set to work.

When Outh'n removed his tunic this time, he tested the tenderness of his ribs under the healing patch and felt nothing more than the normal pressure. Shocked, he peeled away the patch and found no trace of his wound. His hand brushed over it several times in amazement. Surely there should be a scar for such a deep wound. He moved back to the mirror to check the reflection there.

Sure enough, the place looked no different from the rest of his skin. Outh'n checked his cheek again, thinking maybe it'd healed since he'd shaved. His shoulders slumped. The brand still shone an angry reddish-pink, hard scabs still covering the deeper gouges. He shook his head. Hope was a fickle friend. It was best to attempt joy for the wound which healed.

Shaking his head, he stepped into the breeches, finding them a perfect fit, and wrapped the belt around his waist. Checking over his attire one more time, he nodded once and stepped out to meet Kol.

"Ah, I see you figured it out."

"It's something I've worn before, though rarely. These are ceremonial garments worn only during special festivals in my home. The last time I wore such a thing, I was very young. And there's usually a shirt and vest embroidered with bright patterns." Nostalgia cracked his voice.

Kol cocked his head and shrugged. Then he turned with a command. "Follow me."

They were heading in a new direction entirely, and Serafin was nowhere in sight. The broad back in front of him sped away on legs like tree trunks. Outh'n picked up his pace.

"Walk well the path," Kol grumbled.

"Eiya?" What did he mean by that?

"Watch your step," the dark giant enunciated. "It's easy to lose your footing here."

"Ah." Outh'n remembered his passage into the interior. He might not be sure of much in life except being alert. " I'm always watching where I step." 'Whether here or back in Prichud,' he added silently to himself.

For quite some time, silence wrapped around them like a heavy cloak. Leaf litter muffled their footsteps. The hallway varied little, making it difficult to tell how far they'd truly gone.

"How much farther, Kol?"

The answer was so long in coming, Outh'n thought his guide hadn't heard or was ignoring him. His temper flared at the latter thought. He jogged to catch up as he snapped, "Didn't you hear me?"

"I heard," came the gruff reply, "but I'm not obliged to answer your questions."

"What in the name of Tugansol is this?" Outh'n sputtered.

"Just follow me and keep quiet," Kol commanded.

"But—" Outh'n's complaint died abruptly as he tripped over a raised root and almost fell flat on his face. He caught himself just in time.

Kol stopped and turned to face him. When Outh'n's gaze met the dark eyes of his guide, Kol spoke quiet, simple words radiating the promise of swift retribution. "All you have to do is follow me, watch your step, and hold your tongue. Can you manage those simple instructions, Outh'n Durr?"

Outh'n searched the bigger man's eyes for any hint of contempt or condescension. Finding none, he nodded silently.

"Good. Come on." Kol turned and continued down the hallway.

The temptation to speak was certainly a hard one to fight, but he needed to stay here. Outh'n needed to live. He didn't know why he wanted that so badly. Life had seldom been good to him.

"This way," Kol's voice cut into his musings. They turned to the right and met Serafin once again. She stood in the center of an open, airy room similar to the shrine he'd first entered.

Sweat rolled over him, making his skin itch, and he couldn't pull in a full breath. Kol and Serafin seemed untouched by the oppressive heat and humidity.

"You have come far, Outh'n," Serafin said. "Perhaps not as far in the way of some, but certainly farther in others." She spun slowly in the center of the room, raising her arms to take in the entire space. "At Yacan, only those whose determination is stronger than their selfish desires can survive." That fierce blue-green gaze blazed into his own golden-brown one. The Guardian didn't fight to hold his gaze as others did, trying to figure out which eye to look at. She just looked at him. He immediately relaxed, but her next words raised the tension again. "Are you determined? Or is Outh'n Durr selfish?"

Outh'n didn't know how to answer such an odd question, but he had a sneaky suspicion it was the latter. Would exile be his sentence once again, or worse? He gulped and held his tongue. He would have turned away, but her eyes had captured him, unrelenting.

"Well, Outh'n?" One delicate, winged eyebrow lifted.

She expected an answer? Did he speak truth or lie? He had a feeling she would know immediately which was which. If he lied, he'd surely die where he stood. "I have a feeling I might be among the latter, Guardian Serafin," he mumbled, finally able to turn his gaze away.

Soft steps padded closer. She stood so near, their noses would touch if she'd been taller. He stared down into her eyes once again. "The sign of a strong heart is one who speaks truth, no matter what the result might be." She stayed a moment longer, then stepped back. He took a deep breath before realizing this one actually filled his chest. Praise Tugansol!

"Let the trials begin. As you go through each one, Outh'n Durr, be true to yourself and to the Creator who gave you life and sustains you. As long as you do this, you will survive the tests."

The tiny woman turned on her heel and strode down a hallway he hadn't seen before. As soon as she stepped over the arch-framed threshold, a thick curtain of vines descended, shielding her from his view. He turned to face Kol, only to discover the giant was also gone. Spinning around slowly, he took in the room, realizing he was completely alone.

Or maybe they hid, watching him? Only two choices lay before him — wait, or try to find an opening. Before, he'd been told not to touch anything or step anywhere off the main path. He'd been told to remain silent and watch where he placed his feet. This floor seemed solid enough. He stepped forward to cross it and fell through the air. The scream died in his throat. Who'd respond, anyway?

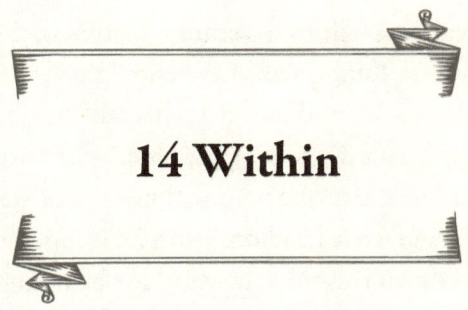

14 Within

Darkness enveloped Outh'n when he opened his eyes, reminding him of his last dawnings at home. How far had he fallen?

"Is anyone there?" He called out, groaning as he rolled onto his hands and knees, then sat back on folded legs. The ground was smooth, no pebbles or ruts dug into his knees or palms, but His whole body ached. He reached out and swept the floor, trying to discover something, anything, that might tell him where he was or what he was supposed to do there. The smooth floor reminded him of stone, but it wasn't as cold as it should be.

Outh'n waited a long time but there was still no answer and he still didn't know what he should do now. After the silenced stretched uncomfortably long and prickles attacked his legs, he got up on his knees and eased forward, sweeping the ground around him as he went. The grit of dirt met his seeking fingers, as well as a few scattered leaves. Nothing more could he find. He crawled forward on his hands and knees, taking care to examine the path before continuing forward. When he'd gone a short distance this way, and his back muscles screamed at him more shrill than the wind in the Wistyng Mountains, he sat back on his haunches and sighed. The new position allowed him to stretch, so he twisted from side to side at the waist, then hugged his knees to his chest.

When his muscles loosened up, he returned to the task. On and on he crawled, pausing periodically to stretch. The grumbling of his stomach finally called a halt to his search. "Is this it, then? You wish to kill me by starvation? Taking away food and light?"

He hissed in disgust and stood to his full height. "I am Outh'n Durr, the wrongly accused, the unjustly hated and misunderstood. But I am also Outh'n Durr, the one who will not die of starvation. If I am meant to die, let me face it head on." And he stepped out in faith that when his foot set down this time, he wouldn't be falling through air.

His suspicion proved true. As soon as his foot touched the ground, light streamed in upon him, blinding him with its intensity. He hissed in pain, squinting against it but trying to keep his eyes on the surrounding area. Tears blurred his vision. It took longer than it should have for his vision to adjust.

When it did, he stood on a dirt path edged by ripply, thick tree trunks and leafy vines dotted here and there with luminescent foliage and blossoms. A fork divided the path ahead of him, so he had a choice. The left path seemed to have fresher air and a bit more light than the right one. He set off at once, ready to be done with these trials.

Before long, he came to a bend in the path which ended in another round room, similar to the one Serafin and Kol had left him in earlier. Only in this one, there were several paths branching off of the central hub, much like the spokes of a cart's wheel.

"So," Outh'n turned slowly to view each one. "Which one is the right one?"

He counted them off, finding nine, and chose the last one. It seemed fitting since everyone chose him last during required group activities. It seemed fitting. Outh'n set off down the path with sure steps. He'd been walking a while when he noticed a creaking sound and heard someone whispering behind him. When he turned to see who or what followed him, instead of a person, a vine curtain settled into place. There was no going back. The vines sealed his only retreat.

Indecision held him in place, and the light dimmed. He started forward again. With each step he took, the light brightened until it seemed the mid-dawning suns shone down on him. As he walked, he recognized the path and, with dread, the tree which lay ahead. Outh'n lifted his eyes to the branches and spotted a golden head of hair and a smile he never thought he'd see again.

"Alanyin," he whispered. What he was seeing wasn't possible, he knew. But the scents and sights, the firm dirt path under his feet, the sound and feel of the breeze made convincing himself hard. Real or not, if he could be with her, he'd stay here forever.

"Alanyin?" he called louder.

"Outh'n," her voice was a mere whisper on the breeze, as if she was further away than she looked.

He ran towards her, knowing what was going to happen. He picked up speed, but the harder he pressed, the slower he became. As if time slowed, Outh'n had no choice but to watch as her dainty, booted foot slipped off the branch she was using to climb down.

"No! Not again," he roared, angered beyond reason. "Alanyin, hang on! I'm coming for you. I'll catch you this time. Trust me and hang on." Her fingers were slipping and he couldn't look away. First one, then another, then the rest slipped away, and she crumpled slowly, silently, irrevocably, into a mangled heap under their tree in their favorite place.

"No——o!" The mournful cry ripped from his throat, the howl of a wild beast joining him as Oowah loped up to the still form. "What is this? What is this, Serafin!" He turned, searching for the Guardian who was certainly behind this nightmare.

His wuveia friend opened powerful jaws as wide as he could and devoured what remained of his love. "No, Oowah. Why?" Outh'n sobbed uncontrollably now, finding it impossible to move, unable to stop the carnage at his feet. He collapsed to his knees and begged Tugansol to stop what he could not. "Please, have mercy, Tugansol. I can't! Not again."

The hunting party took him by surprise as they sped past blades raised and war cries rending the air. Outh'n could only watch as they hacked Oowah to pieces, destroying his companion, who had only been faithful. Is this what had happened to him? What Bazhbet couldn't bring himself to say only days ago in Chefvna? Why was Serafin showing him these things?

When they were done with Oowah, the hunting party turned on him with malice, eyes glittering with evil anticipation.

"Traitor!" yelled one.

"Kill him!" More took up the cry.

"He deserves to die!"

"Murderer!" The last voice was the only familiar one. Kurg'l was among them. Leading them straight to him with his bare blade raised high, bitter hatred hardened his eyes. He sneered as he got close. "Try to escape now, Outh'n Durr," he hissed.

Those words incensed Outh'n. Waiting until the last second, he jumped up with all his strength. Since he expected to fight against his own heaviness, the violence of his push was more powerful than he expected, lifting him clean off the ground. His elbow met with Kurg'l's jaw and the larger man's head snapped back viciously. But Outh'n didn't stop there. He steeled himself and fought his way through all the attackers. Their blades bit and slashed, but he didn't care. Everyone he loved was dead, by their hands, and the desire for vengeance overshadowed all else.

One man swept him off his feet with the butt of a spear and the next thing he knew, pain flared everywhere as the group stabbed him in unity. He cried out, angry, frustrated, "Why, Tugansol? Do you hate me so much?"

The men only jeered as he fell deeper and deeper into oblivion. Before he lost consciousness, a whisper brushed past his ear. "You are not hated, and there are those who love you still."

15 New

His skin stung, the searing of fire. Outh'n jerked awake. Wide-eyed, he searched left and right for the attackers. He couldn't find them. The tree, Alanyin, Oowah — all were gone as if they'd never existed. He patted his chest, arms, and legs. Not a single wound remained. But the stinging in his cheek was relentless. He reached up to touch the bloody, raw place on the right side of his face and whimpered when his hand came away covered in gore. He stood, stumbled, righted himself and trudged forward, unsure where he was going.

He came upon his old home, recognizing none of the surroundings. Tripping up the stairs, he crossed the wide porch and opened the door.

"Moyri? Babeiya? Ailiin?" There was no answer, so he tried again. "Are you here? I need help, Moyri. Something's happened."

A shuffle in the far corner drew his attention. Ailiin stood backed into the corner, wielding a kitchen blade against him, her eyes wide with fright.

"Who are you?" Her voice trembled and his heart broke.

"It's me, Outh'n." His own voice cracked and his eyes burned with tears. "Don't you recognize me, Ailiin? It's your own iyaba." His voice faded to a broken, whispered plea. He slowly lifted one hand, palm upturned to her, but stayed where he was. "Please, Ailiin, I need your help."

"I don't have an iyaba. Not anymore." Spittle flew from her mouth, and she brandished the blade in front of her, both hands wrapped around the wooden grip. "My iyaba wouldn't have left me in the hands of Kurg'l. My iyaba died when he walked away from me."

Shock rendered him frozen. Then he lowered his hand, his shoulders slumping. "I didn't do that, Ailiin. You know I had to leave. And I sent the message to warn you. You know I wouldn't just leave and forget. I love you and Moyri and Babeiya. You are all in my heart until I draw my last breath." Still, she held the blade at the ready. "Please believe me, Ailiin. Please."

Slowly, Ailiin lowered the blade. Halfway between where she'd been holding it in front of her and having it rest against her side, a shadowy blur sped past Outh'n, startling him. Before he knew it, Kurg'l had his sadau trapped against him. The blade now threatened to pierce her neck.

"Iyaba, if it's really you, help me," Ailiin pleaded. Her eyes widened once again in fright.

Outh'n scanned the room, looking for anything he could use to free her.

"It's no use, Murderer," Kurg'l sneered. "There's nothing you can do to stop me." And in the blink of an eye, he slit Ailiin's throat. Tossing her aside, he gave Outh'n no time to even think about what just happened. "Your turn, you son-of-a-silti."

Outh'n's focus sharpened, and he braced himself. Anger stirred in his belly, an uncontrollable blaze. "You'll pay for that, Kurg'l."

Kurg'l's menacing laugh sliced through the air as he charged, plunging the blade deep into Outh'n's core. Where there had been blazing heat, icy cold rushed in and Outh'n slumped to the floor.

"WHAT'S GOING ON, SERAFIN?" he growled. Tears left tracks on his cheeks as he rolled onto his side, once again blinded by shadows.

"Isn't it enough? I've lost my family once. Why must I live through it again in a worse way than what truly happened? I don't understand."

"You will, Outh'n Durr." The voice was a shivering whisper, soothing like a cool breeze on a muggy day. Whoever it was, the voice didn't belong to Serafin. "The one who endures to the end is a true victor."

Outh'n snorted in disbelief. Something stung his cheek. "Ow! What was that?"

"Listen carefully, Outh'n Durr," the voice spoke again. "I know your pain, understand what you have endured. I'll share your burden if you will share mine."

"What do you mean?"

"Exactly what I say. When you need to speak to someone of your struggle, I will gladly listen. In exchange, I need powerful warriors. I believe you would be a good one."

He snorted again. "Why would you want someone whose own village rejected him without cause? I must be defective somehow or they would never have done such a thing to me."

"Your people could not see past their own selfishness to see the beauty of your spirit. I can."

Outh'n was silent for a long while. "What's the alternative?"

"Death."

Outh'n laughed outright, though there was no humor in it. "Death is inevitable for us all, isn't it?"

He sensed agreement, though he couldn't explain how. When there was no other answer, he rose slowly to his feet. "Alright then. I accept this trade."

"Are you certain? There is no going back."

"I'm certain. What do I need to do?"

"Choose one, Outh'n Durr." A dim light illuminated three goblets exquisitely crafted of pale wood on a low table before him. "Choose one and drink the contents."

"What's in them?"

"Do you not trust me?"

"I don't even know you."

A breathy chuckle filled his mind. "This is true. I give you my word the contents will not kill you, though I thought it didn't matter to you."

Outh'n shrugged, then nodded. "Does it matter which one?"

"In a way. Your choice will determine your service."

Outh'n walked to the table. Each goblet held a different colored liquid — pale green, pale blue, and a dark color that could've been anything. He grabbed the pale green, thinking it looked most like his moyri's herbal tea. He downed it in one go.

"Well chosen, Outh'n Durr. Welcome to Yacan. I am Edrea."

And then the burning sensation returned, low at first but steadily building. "What have you done to me?" Outh'n doubled over as he cried out. Falling to his knees, he succumbed to oblivion.

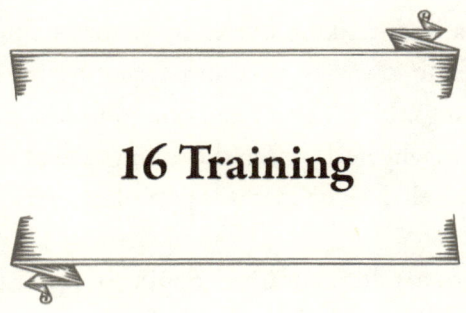

16 Training

Outh'n dodged, but not quick enough to avoid Kol's staff. He'd have a nice bruise on his left bicep and a strained left hamstring. A frustrated growl rumbled through his chest.

"None of that, Outh'n," a rich alto voice chided from outside the sparring platform. The Genzetti female who'd spoken was shorter and smaller than Kol, but far larger than any female of his previous acquaintance. As if that wasn't eye-catching enough, her skin, hair, and eyes were a deep violet, whereas Kol was shadowy black. He'd learned quickly that when people described Genzetti as "colorful," they meant something other than what he'd imagined.

"You don't command me, Eiva Di'Amo. Keep your comments to yourself," he snapped, spitting on the ground in frustration.

"Focus, Outh'n," Kol recalled his attention. A thump of his teacher's staff reverberated through the platform.

Outh'n's own weapon of choice was a shorter spear tipped with a thin, leaf-shaped blade. He'd honed the edge until it was sharp enough to split a hair. At first, Outh'n was reluctant to spar with bladed weapons. But Kol's point was a good one. If you weren't good enough to survive sparring with live weapons, you were better off dead than holding all the others back.

When he woke from the darkness Edrea's drink had dropped him into, Kol had been squatting nearby with a change of clothes, already ordering him around. Outh'n knew Kol, being a resident of Yacan for longer, set him higher in rank. He'd been told later that the Genzetti had once been a high-ranking officer in Genzet's elite fighting force, the Ver'therin. Still, knowing that and accepting his leadership were two different things. He'd never been one to follow the rule of others blindly, which was why he'd chosen the solitary life of a glashiin worker. He scoffed at himself. Maybe that was part of the reason he'd ended up here.

A sharp tap to his shin sent him hopping backward. Eiva chuckled, but Kol frowned. "If you don't want to take this seriously, then maybe you should let someone replace you on the platform," the latter remarked, lifting one corner of his black lips in a sneer which bared one fang.

Outh'n reset his stance for battle. "Not a chance, Genzetti." He'd also learned more about the proper way to stand up for oneself since his training had begun. His temper still got the better of him from time to time, but he was learning. He had Kol to thank for those lessons, too.

Back and forth across the platform, wood and metal clacked, thumped, and chimed, the sounds carrying through the canopy. By the time they finished, a gash bled over Outh'n's left eye. Both shoulders sported bruises, as well as many places across his back. The left side of his ribs ached, and a red, swollen knot on his right shin begged the cool, soothing waters of the stream near his home. Muscles he never knew he had screamed with burning pain of strain. With a sinking feeling, he admitted to himself waking up would be hard when the sunslight gleamed through the windows of his tiny cabin the next dawning.

Outh'n's stay in the byrnir, the alehouse and inn at the center of the market square, only lasted several dawnings until his cabin was available. It had been comfortable, but when he saw his own dwelling, a sense of belonging rolled over him. Small it might be, but it was his own home and something he'd never thought to have since tiav'yag couldn't own property. They never stayed in one place very long, anyway. Most villages wouldn't even let them set foot inside their borders, urging them on in the vilest of ways.

Edrea had saved Outh'n from an awful fate and well he knew it. If his service in life was the trade for having a place to belong and put his skills to good use, he was more than willing. He trudged to his home now in the fading light of the suns when he heard a stealthy step behind him. He crouched and spun on his heel. A splash of purple, difficult to see for certain in the dimness, caught his eye for a moment.

"Eiva Di'Amo, did you need something from me?" He relaxed his stance, watching the place where he'd spotted the small patch of color. He put as much confidence as possible into his tone. He'd learned early on both guards and trainees had little respect for those who hung back. That had been hard to get used to. Sometimes he came upon a behavior that was frowned upon at home but rewarded here, making him wonder if this place could be more of a home than Prichud had ever been. "Eiva, are you following me? Did Kol put you up to it?"

"As if he would stoop to such a thing for a trifling Shinnoahn youngling," she sneered, and strode out of the shrubs where she'd hidden.

"Then why are you here, trying to hide from me?" He crossed his arms over his chest, light enough to loosen them in defense if necessary, and cocked his head to one side without bothering to hide his hated eye. Another thing he'd learned since coming to Yacan, oddities could be a confusing distraction during battle.

"I am here, Outh'n Durr, because I feel you show promise." She mimicked his stance, no trace of a smile remaining on her face.

After a moment, Outh'n snorted in derision. "Whatever you say, Genzetti. It's been a long day. I'm tired and sore. I'm going home." He turned and started back down the path.

"You hateful little wretch," Eiva hissed behind him, incensed. "How dare you spurn my help, the help of one who is your superior in every way?"

His hackles raised at her haughtiness. She'd only arrived at Yacan a nainda or two ahead of him. Tightening his muscles, he readied himself to take on her challenge.

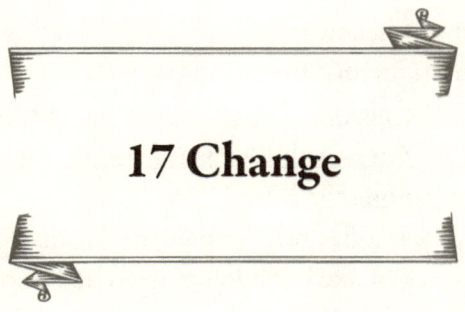

17 Change

O r at least he'd thought he was ready. Something stung first one calf muscle, then the other, and his legs gave out beneath him.

"What have you done, Eiva Di'Amo?" Outh'n bared his teeth at her and growled. He wondered at his tendency to call upon memories of Oowah at the peak of his anger. "You're going to regret that."

"Oh?" When Eiva smiled, it was rarely warm or inviting. She saved those for Kol, who repeatedly ignored them. Now, though, the ice in her glare froze the blood in his veins. What was she planning? "And how will you do anything sprawled on the ground like a gurba searching blindly for a rotting seed?" she jeered.

Outh'n seethed. By the time he noticed the burning in his belly, it had spread almost the length of his extremities. "Eiva, you need to leave now. I don't want you here and I don't want trouble. I just want to go home and rest." The words were a struggle and his eyes burned, though not with tears this time. A stirring of the ground beneath him took his eyes from the Genzetti warrior. "What in the name—" But before he could finish, Edrea's roots trapped and held him.

Eiva stood nearby, a relaxed observer, but not near enough to become entangled. She laughed, a scornful sound that set his blood boiling to match the burn flooding his nerve endings. He tried to speak, but the sounds he emitted resembled more of what he'd heard from Oowah. He frowned. Was this Edrea's doing?

Eiva drew back, her blade raised high. Outh'n closed his eyes, resigned to his fate, when he felt a thump. His eyes flashed open to find

Eiva in a similar predicament. He wanted to laugh so badly, but the vines holding him tightened in warning.

"This will not be pleasant for either of you, but I cannot give this gift any other way. You have both earned something extra which will allow you to excel among the Myrr."

Edrea's words cut off, and the pain intensified. He snarled and writhed as his bones creaked and joints stretched beyond their limits. His skin prickled as if an army of metcha feasted on him endlessly. He howled in impotent pain, shocked at how like Oowah he sounded. Had he paid closer attention than he'd thought?

As suddenly as it had come, the pain disappeared, leaving him worn like an old cleansing scrap and gasping for breath. Eiva sounded no better, but he kept his eyes closed as he focused on regaining his energy. The soft pad of a beast's paw had him springing to his feet before he was really ready. He wobbled, then righted himself, scanning the area.

A black beast with a short snout and needle-like fangs stood before him. Its black eyes seemed vaguely familiar. The wide tufted ears twitched, searching for the smallest sound. Outh'n froze, waiting for the moment he must defend himself against such a fierce foe. Great Giver of Life! This beast had shoulders like a mountain and legs like tree trunks.

"There are three vesat," the beast spoke into his mind with a voice as familiar as the eyes blinking at him.

"No," whispered Outh'n. "Kol? Is that you?"

The beast nodded. "Stop interrupting Outh'n Durr and listen. There are three vesat. We are of the first. This form is called vesat'ya, warriors who shift into land beast forms."

Outh'n held out a hand to stop the unbelievable words. Surprise arrested his thoughts when he saw a massive paw covered in fur where he expected his own hand to be.

Kol continued, oblivious to his confusion. "The Ammir has asked me to train you two in using your forms. While I'm certain I can help

Outh'n," he turned that massive head to where Outh'n knew Eiva had been, "Eiva, your form differs greatly from ours. I will ask for someone familiar with prey forms to aid you in learning of the tools your form hides."

He turned, his long tail striped with dark gray, swished back and forth as if he was impatient. "Both of you follow me," he said without a backward glance.

Outh'n turned to look at Eiva, who struggled to rise on spindly legs which were a mottled blend of muddy purple, green, and gold. Two curving horns jutted out of her elongated snout. Fuzzy, leaf-shaped ears the size of his palm twitched and swiveled above each dark eye. A fringe of long, thick lashes ringed her eyes and a long, thin tail tipped with a fuzzy tuft matched her ears and swung back and forth in a strange rhythm. Once she regained her footing, she stamped one cloven hoof in fury and snorted, shaking her horned head. She almost toppled over for her efforts. Outh'n would've laughed, but he was having his own issues getting used to his new form.

"Be easy Outh'n Durr. Relax into this form and reach your potential."

"My thanks, Edrea. I'll do that." He snorted, but it came out as a huff.

Outh'n set off following Kol, slowly at first, then building speed until he was trotting at an easy lope.

The tappity-tap of hooves on leaf-mold followed him. Awkward and often accompanied by an enraged snort, Eiva drew steadily nearer.

"I can't believe she turned me into prey," Eiva's alto mutter interrupted Outh'n's concentration.

"Edrea chooses as befits the host, Eiva," Kol chided. "Focus on honing your skills in that form. She gave you what you would need and your form is important to the whole of Yacan." Kol stopped and spun on his back legs to face them. Outh'n almost toppled over in his efforts to not slam into Kol. Eiva didn't fare so well, tripped by her graceful legs.

Kol padded closer and stood over her, looking down his nose. Outh'n tensed, but stayed where he was. "Are you dissatisfied, Eiva Di'Amo?"

It was a long while coming, and at that, begrudgingly, but she finally shook her head, setting the tufts at her ear-tips fluttering. Outh'n wondered at her form. He'd never seen a beast like that in Shinnoah. But then again, he'd seen nothing like Kol's form, either.

"Good. Rise and let's get moving. We have much to learn and little time to learn it."

Kol waited, tail continuously twitching, ears swiveling to note Eiva's rising and make certain both followed obediently. Then he set off once again down the path.

18 Alert

If Outh'n thought the training had been difficult before, doing the same in his vesat form was tougher. He'd suspected what his form was because of his paw and how he'd sounded when he tried to speak. But it wasn't until he saw his reflection in a calm pool that he totally understood the depth of his transformation. Where Oowah had been the mottled colors of a Shinnoahn forest, Outh'n was a dark brown with tawny and pale gray highlights scattered here and there, as if an annoyed artist threw his brush. His eyes remained their normal color, just as Kol's and Eiva's had, though Eiva's pupils had changed shape to slanted, knobby lines. Kol's also changed to horizontal, pointed ellipses, but they continually widened to circles and shrunk back to the ellipses, as befit his beast.

When Kol made his announcement to both him and Eiva right after their first shift, Outh'n had groaned in dismay. But if he was honest, Kol was a thorough teacher, even if he was strict. He'd learned, too, the word for teacher in the Genzet tongue was 'iteik'I.' Kol was adamant he be called by that designation. The word for student was 'eik'it' and he reminded Outh'n of his lower status often.

At first the younger man was angry about the forced distinction, and it cost him in all of his early skirmishes with the shadow-black karyna. Kol laughed at his mishaps, but catching the iteik'i off guard was impossible, especially when Outh'n's enhanced vision was clouded by fury.

He finally realized Kol was angering him on purpose. Outh'n could've kicked himself that dawning.

"Well done, Outh'n," Kol's voice rumbled with pride. "It's about time, too. I wondered if you'd ever catch on."

Outh'n just shook his head and snorted, not deigning to reply. He jumped right back into the fight, determined to win the dawning.

Over the next few sessions, the two sparred furiously, each trying to best the other. Outh'n lost over and over, but he was definitely improving. He pushed Kol to improvise more than once by the end of the latest training session.

The two warriors, now in human form, followed the circular rope and plank stair down from the raised platform and collapsed when they reached the forest floor. That was another thing Outh'n had to get used to — wearing minimal clothes. Shifting to the vesat form wasn't kind to outer garments, so Edrea provided special undergarments for each warrior gifted with vesat. It wasn't much, but covered the important bits well. In an actual fight, if one had to shift quickly, there would be no need to worry about vulnerability.

As much clothing as Shinnoahn people wore, that was probably the hardest thing for Outh'n to get used to. He learned the Bot'hani didn't like it much, either. Funny how so many tsimikin of being taught every clan was too different to get along, and yet here was a colony of people from every corner of Y'Dahnndrya who worked together and played together in relative harmony. Outh'n was truly coming to love his new home.

"You've improved so much today, Outh'n," Kol said with confidence, pulling him away from his wandering thoughts. "I actually wonder what took you so long."

The genuine quality in his voice and the words put Outh'n at ease, so he answered honestly, keeping the details brief. "I don't know. In my village, when I'd fight back, it made the fight last longer and meant more pain for me."

"You don't have that luxury here, eik'it. You'll need to stay alert, always be ready to fight back with everything you've got. This isn't a scuffle between younglings. It's a fight for your life and the life of your people."

"I understand." Outh'n looked Kol directly in the eye for a change.

"Do you, Outh'n Durr? Do you really?" Skepticism tainted the words this time, and a scowl darkened the older man's brow.

Outh'n huffed and rose. "Look, iteik'I," he gestured with one hand as he spoke, "You asked. I answered as honestly as I could. What more do you want from me?"

"The same thing Edrea wants from you."

"And that is," he left the words dangling in the air between them.

"Loyalty. Honesty. Integrity. And your determination to put all of yourself into protecting our home, our benefactor, and our people."

"You've got that, Kol. What else can I do to prove it to you?"

"Having witnessed your performance until now, you wish me to believe you're committed after a couple of successful sparring sessions?"

Outh'n stared at him for a long while before daring to speak, the words burning on his tongue. He finally settled on the least offensive, having no desire to anger the man who'd felled him again and again, dawning after dawning. "I see your point."

Kol nodded once. "Good. If you want to prove yourself, it takes more than that. It's good to know you understand."

OUTH'N HAD A LOT TO consider as he hiked back to his little cabin. With the light steadily fading, he drifted off the path without realizing it. By the time he noticed what he'd done, he was on some little-used trail. He chided himself for his lack of focus and wondered what to do. Did he dare try finding his way back to the main trail, or did he just stay put for the duration of the dusking?

A rustling in the shrubs nearby had him shifting in the blink of an eye. His vision improved, and he thanked Tugansol for the wuveia's special gift of seeing in the dark and their enhanced sense of smell. He scanned the trail, sniffed the ground in front of him, testing the new tools he hadn't tried out yet. Turning about on the trail, he found he could retrace his steps easily.

The underbrush shivered again, and this time, he caught sight of the reason. A thorny vine trapped a small burrower. The pull to attack was so strong, he was creeping toward it before he recognized what was happening. He shook his head, trotted over to the vine and nipped through it with his jaws, setting the smaller beast free with a mental apology.

Shaking his shaggy head once more, he set back to work, finding his way home. Despite having found the main trail again, he still couldn't shake the feeling of being followed. It was time to end this farce.

Outh'n darted off the path through a small opening in the underbrush and doubled back down the trail. It wasn't long before he scented something different. He'd never encountered such a strong, salty scent before now. It could've been because of his heightened sense of smell in his current form. The only other reason was he'd stumbled upon something he hadn't yet seen on Yacan.

Should he track this unknown being? Should he call for help? Maybe he should just go home. It had been a long dawning, and he was tired. There was no way to know if this thing was something he could handle on his own or not. And who knew if anyone would hear him out here?

A bubbly gurgle was the only warning he had before two slimy, webbed claws grabbed for his hind legs. If it hadn't been for his quick reflexes, his life could've ended there. He spun, looking everywhere for the creature's body, but the only thing he could see was a single pair of claws, opening and closing, extending and retracting.

The movement intrigued him, and he watched closely, waiting for the next attack. Open and shut, forward and back, the slow drip of muck, all worked together to lull him into a state of half-sleep.

When the attack came, Outh'n was in no shape to defend himself. Cold claws of death ringed his paws and dragged him under the leaf-strewn floor of the forest. He barely had the sense to howl before his snout went under.

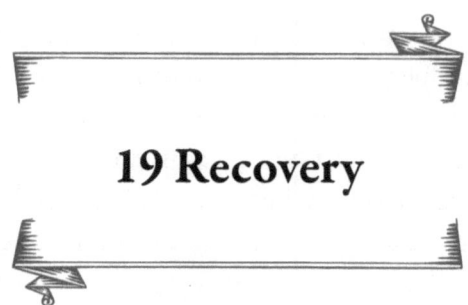

19 Recovery

Outh'n's waking was slow and painful. The realm of oblivion tempted him to sink back into sleep, whispering promises of freedom from the hurt. He groaned.

"He wakes," a cracking voice murmured somewhere behind his head. "Now I can determine the extent of the damage."

A rough shove against his shoulder set him howling in anger and fear. He wanted to curl into a ball and hide, but any movement sent the fire of the suns racing through his muscles. He whined, deep in his throat as Oowah might have done. Words refused to form as pain crowded out everything in its mad rush to consume him.

"Calm down, Outh'n Durr," the voice, like wind-stirred leaves, filled his mind, calming the wild storm his injuries caused. "The healer and I will do what we can for you. Quiet your mind by focusing on your purpose."

Whip-like vines wrapped around Outh'n's torso and both of his legs. Tiny pins pricked his skin as Edrea sought the root of the problem. "I am sorry, Outh'n Durr, that you ventured within reach of the kre'li. He wanders where he will. I clearly mark the paths for reasons such as this."

Outh'n tried to nod, tried to think of the process when the creature had grabbed him.

"Do not exert yourself," Edrea's voice soothed as her inspection continued. "I have discovered what I needed to know. You will soon sleep. When you wake again, the pain will have faded somewhat."

Though everything he heard since waking confused him, Outh'n finally managed a coherent thought he could express in words. "Thank you, Edrea, but why would you do this for me?"

"Because Outh'n Durr," she responded with a tinge of humor, "you have heart for one so heavily burdened with trials. You are a fighter, a powerful fighter. Yacan needs you." There was a brief pause before she added, "I need warriors like you, Outh'n. Please do not put yourself in danger needlessly."

He felt the depth of her concern deep within his mind and wondered at it.

"Be calm now. It will sting and though it seems like forever, the cure is quick to take effect."

With no further warning, white-hot fire filled every part of him, radiated from every pore. He cried out before the blackness claimed him once more.

WHEN NEXT HE WOKE, it was to pounding. He'd thought at first that it was his head that ached. It took quite some time to realize he was in his own humzek and someone was pounding on his door.

"I'm coming," Eiva groused from his side. "Hold it down for the injured." In a snide murmur, she added, "What gurba has no care for the ill?" Why was Eiva in his cabin?

"Ah, Iteik'i Kol," her voice switched immediately, radiating charm. Outh'n frowned and tried to rise. His muscles refused to cooperate. "What brings you here on this fine evening?"

"How is he?" Kol's gruff tone was at odds with the words of concern.

"Always to the point, eiya?" Eiva chuckled. The velvety tones reminded him of Alanyin's laughter, even though they were so different.

"Enough, Eiva Di'Amo," Kol snapped. "I asked you a question."

"Yes, Iteik'i Kol Udota," she hissed back at him. In a smoother, though still formal tone, she added, "Outh'n Durr is recovering and has just woken up." She waved a hand toward his humzek. "As you can see, I assume?"

Kol snorted in annoyance and pushed past her. "Outh'n? Is she right? Are you well?"

Outh'n stared at his sparring partner and teacher. In a hoarse voice he hardly recognized, he answered, "She's not lying to you. My muscles aren't cooperating yet and I hurt, but it's better than it was before."

Kol sank to his knees. "Thanks be to Andurdrao," he murmured as his palms covered his face.

Outh'n turned startled eyes to Eiva, who shrugged and shook her head, setting her beaded braids in motion. "Iteik'i Kol?" he asked. When Kol still said nothing, he prompted him again and asked, "What's going on?"

"I failed my eik'it, Outh'n Durr." The murmur was further muffled by Kol's hands, until he rubbed his face, then dropped his them into his lap. He raised tormented black orbs to meet Outh'n's amazed stare. "Never have I ever done such a despicable thing in all the years I spent training eik'itin. Why Edrea hasn't punished me yet is a mystery." The dark depths of self-loathing in his gaze shocked Outh'n, who had thought he was alone in suffering that trait. He flicked a glance to Eiva, who stared at Kol, one eyebrow raised.

"I assure you, Iteik'i Kol, I'm fine." He thought a moment, then amended his declaration to better reflect the truth. "Well, I will be. Hopefully soon."

"It doesn't change the fact that you received an injury while under my care. You are my charge. I am responsible for you."

Outh'n's jaw tightened. He had plenty to say, but this must be something about the way Genzet Clan ran things. "Forgive me, Iteik'i, but is this Genzet or Yacan? Perhaps Edrea hasn't punished you because she does things differently here."

Kol's scowl deepened. "You are right, but her methods change nothing in my heart. My own beliefs about personal conduct and duty aren't so easily changed."

Eiva laughed. The peals of laughter jangled Outh'n's nerves. Why she was even here was still a mystery to him. "Kol Udota, Iteik'i, you are most amusing."

"You find duty to be something humorous?" A warning permeated the growled query.

Maybe she missed the darkening of Kol's brow, but Outh'n had not. "That's..." But what could he say to two Genzetti warriors who were not even his friends and only his allies through Edrea's bond? It was his house, though. If they wanted to fight, he'd rather they do it outside. "If you both insist on arguing, could you do it outside my home, please?" He kept his tone as respectful as possible, but allowed some of the exhaustion to seep into the words.

Kol nodded briskly and his footsteps thudded across the wooden floor, muting temporarily when they crossed his colorful woven-grass rug. The door swung open. As fast as Kol had arrived, he departed. Eiva followed quickly. He'd have to ask her when he saw her next, why she was in his home without his permission.

20 Friends

Five nainda later, Outh'n's body bore no more signs of the kre'li attack, visible or otherwise. The headaches had passed, and he started sparring with Kol again. Neither of them spoke of the larger man's visit to his home, but Outh'n often wondered what went on in his iteik'i's mind.

Only a moment's musing. That's all it took for Kol to win this skirmish. He swiped Outh'n's legs out from under him with his long staff, then stood tall beside his prone form.

"What's bothering you today, Outh'n? It's been a while since I've felled you that easily." Disappointment tainted his words.

Outh'n grimaced, then rose slowly to his feet. "My apologies, Iteik'i Kol. You're right. I need to stay focused. Let's go again."

They started again, ending after a brief clacking of weapons when Outh'n lost again.

"Alright. That's it. You're done for the dawning. I refuse to spar with someone so half-hearted and weak-minded." No hint of teasing colored Kol's tone and Outh'n berated himself.

"I can do this, iteik'I. I can. It's just," he paused not knowing how to continue, or even if he should.

"Just what, eik'it? Spit it out before it calls death down upon you."

"Why did you come to my cabin that dawning? You did nothing to me. You didn't command the kre'li to attack me." Outh'n shook his head and leaned on his spear. "I just don't understand why you feel responsible."

"Duty is duty. In Genzet, when one takes on the responsibility of training another, that person's life is their responsibility. If harm comes to their charge, or an eik'it dies while still under their care, the punishment can be as simple as extra labors or as dire as banishment. Depending on the severity of the dereliction of duty, the punishment could be death."

"But this isn't Genzet," Outh'n pressed, eager for Kol to go back to being himself. "Edrea doesn't play by those rules, no matter how you feel about it, iteik'I."

"I know." He growled the acknowledgment, then repeated, "But it doesn't make me feel any better about the kre'li attack. So," the big man paused long enough to set Outh'n's hair on end.

"So?" What was he going to say next?

"So I will escort you home from sparring lessons from this dawning until you have nothing else to learn from me."

Outh'n stiffened and stared at Kol for a long time. He was not pleased. "Do I look like an infant to you?"

"Absolutely not." Kol's braids swung with the force of his motion. He held up one hand, stopping Outh'n as he opened his mouth to reply. "I simply mean, I will walk with you because two warriors are better equipped to fight a surprise attack than one."

Outh'n waited, trying to gauge the truth in the statement. Unfortunately, he waited long enough for them to be joined by Eiva.

"What goes on here, Outh'n? Kol?" Her words attempted to soothe but did nothing to settle Outh'n.

"Kol thinks I'm an infant that needs help." He raised his chin in derision and snorted.

Kol growled, "I already told you that wasn't the case, Outh'n Durr."

"I still don't see it that way."

"But just because you don't see it that way doesn't mean my words are untruths." Genuine confusion wrinkled Kol's brow.

Outh'n suddenly softened his tone, and one corner of his mouth lifted in a crooked grin. "I know that to be so and I accept it as truth. Why can't you also accept your own words, iteik'I?"

Kol thought back over what they'd been discussing and frowned. "Who is the iteik'i here?"

Outh'n wiggled his eyebrows and grinned. "You are. But you really should start acting more like one." He risked a wink at Eiva, who grinned back at him.

"So you two are pairing up against me?" Kol demanded.

Eiva's rich purple faded to a dusky lilac. So Genzetti paled as well? That was an interesting thing to watch.

"No, iteik'I," Outh'n answered. "Eiva has been trying to tell you the same thing for some time, but you refused to listen. I coaxed the truth from your own mouth. We aren't conspiring against you, as you seem to imagine." The thought left a sour taste in Outh'n's mouth.

"Outh'n speaks the truth. I would never be a part of any plot to harm you or your reputation, Kol Udota. I respect you too much." Eiva's declaration was a bit overdone, Outh'n thought, but it seemed to have the desired effect. Kol spent a moment thinking, then nodded.

Outh'n's thought as he left the sparring later was a repetitive lament. "Friendship is so hard."

TWO THUMPS ON HIS DOOR startled Outh'n and steaming kafkhet splattered onto his burled-wood counter. The swirling pattern was one of his favorite things in his cabin, and he shined it to perfection every chance he got. Muttering under his breath, he cleaned the mess as he called out, "Hold on, Eiva. I'm on my way."

Annoyed, he downed the rest of the warm, brewed drink and bounded out the door. "What are we doing today that's got you so excited?" One corner of his lips turned up in wry humor at the twinkle in his friend's eyes.

"Shopping." Her jovial one-word answer wiped the smile off his face in an instant.

"You made me spill my kafkhet for a life-forsaken shopping trip?"

His frown had no effect on her excitement. "Yes. I need your help."

"My help?" Outh'n asked, incredulous.

"Yes. I have something special planned, and I need to look special."

"And you want my opinion?" Outh'n couldn't believe his fashion-conscious friend would ask anyone's opinion, much less a man who often wore only pants and old boots. For her sake, he'd donned a yellow tunic and a black vest embroidered with bright flowers and vines. He also wore his best boots.

"Well, who else am I supposed to ask?" He found her exasperation perversely pleasing after being tricked out of his own plans for the day.

"One of your other friends? One with more curves than me?" He carved a basic female shape in the air between them.

"In case you hadn't noticed, Outh'n Durr, other females are jealous of me." She sounded truly miffed, and Outh'n decided the outing could end up being fun. Maybe.

"Jealous of you?"

"How can you not have noticed?"

"Oh, I don't know. I've been a little busy trying not to be killed by a big Genzetti male who looks and moves like a shadow and happens to also be my iteik'I. Speaking of Kol, he's annoyed with me."

At the mention of his teacher, Eiva stiffened. Ah! So that's what this was all about. Even better.

"So, ah, something special related to Kol, then?"

Eiva simply bobbed her head once.

When she still kept silent, he asked, "So what are we shopping for exactly?"

"Everything," she beamed, as if he'd given her all five of Y'Dahnndrya's moons on a platter.

"Everything?" That sounded ominous.

"New clothes, new hairstyle, new beads and metal baubles — all new." She ticked the items off on her fingers. "I must look my best when I approach him."

Outh'n had his doubts about the outcome, but decided he'd help. It might be fun to see Kol driven to speechlessness by his friend's beauty.

"Alright. I'm no expert, but I know what I like. Maybe he'll like something similar," though Outh'n knew he and Kol didn't seem to like the same things in most cases.

They strolled down the path, mostly in silence, enjoying the symphony of life surrounding them. The suns were still on the rise when they entered the central market area, but Eiva headed directly to a bauble shop. This was one shop Outh'n didn't mind visiting. The items reminded him of home and the few happy times he remembered, most of them with his family and Alanyin.

"What are you looking for here?" he asked as she led him deeper into the shop.

"These." Eiva pointed to a small bowl filled with brilliantly colored glashiin beads. He smiled. "Ah!" she exclaimed. "I knew it!" She carefully chose several beads in deep blue with a purple flash, solid shiny black, and a shimmery golden yellow.

"What are you going to do with them?"

Somewhat distracted, she answered. "They're for my hair, of course."

"Of course," he echoed, smirking.

"Outh'n, if you didn't want to be here, you could've just said no." The corners of her lips turned down and displeasure darkened her tone.

He raised an eyebrow and asked, "Really?"

She beamed, baring both of her fangs. The feral quality made her point clear, especially when paired with eyebrows dipping sharply above her nose.

"I didn't think so." Outh'n crossed his arms over his chest as he scanned the other items nearby. "What about one of these?" He pointed to a black glashiin medallion embossed with a silvery moon.

"Are you serious?" Disgust tainted her lovely visage and Outh'n frowned, too.

"Look, I was just trying to help. You've chosen black beads. I thought this matched."

"Yes, the colors do, but, Outh'n, that's Dahl. Min, the blue moon, is most coveted in our art and decorations. Min is the symbol of Genzet. To wear Dahl—" She left the sentence hanging, but he understood, having seen how important tradition and duty were to her and Kol alike.

"My apologies." He scanned again and found a purple one embossed with one of Edrea's round, single-petaled blossoms. He picked it up. It was very well done. He wondered who the artisan was. "What about this one?" he murmured half-heartedly. If she didn't want it, he did.

"Let me see," she demanded as she reached for it. He held it away from her. When she faced him, confusion was all he could read. She really didn't understand courtesy in the least. He slowly passed it to her.

"It's polite to ask. You never know. I might have wanted to purchase it."

Eiva laughed, but uncertainty tainted it. "You? What would you do with a piece of jewelry like this?"

"Jewelry like this is good for many things. I don't have to wear it to enjoy it."

Eiva stared, open-mouthed, then snapped her jaw shut. She hissed, "You're ridiculous and just angry with me for snatching it."

"Maybe I am. And maybe I'm also tired of helping you shop." He stepped around her to make good on his threat. She grabbed his elbow.

"My apologies, Outh'n. I really didn't think you would want anything in this shop."

He looked at her, then turned his gaze to her hand on his elbow. Staring pointedly, he held his tongue until she let go, then raised his gaze to meet hers. "I'll be up front when you're ready."

He walked toward the door, intending to wait on a bench out in the fresh air. A shop keeper called out, "Is there anything in particular you need, honored customer? I hate for you to leave empty-handed."

Outh'n stopped and thought. If they sold glashiin ornamentation here, perhaps they also sold the supplies for making them. "I was actually wondering if you sold glashiin pieces for working."

The shop-keep beamed. "Why, yes! We have several bags you can choose from in many weights and shapes."

Outh'n smiled. Finally, he could do something with his spare time that wouldn't land him in trouble.

21 Connection

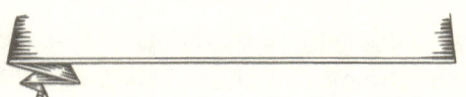

"I still can't believe you bought three bags of leavings. What are you going to do with it all?" Eiva's arms dripped with shopping bags like her tone dripped with disdain. She was busy checking to be sure the shop-keep drew the strings tight enough to keep crawlies and damp from ruining her purchases.

"You'll see," Outh'n smiled as his own bag of goodies swung from the hand furthest away from her. He couldn't believe Tugansol had smiled on him so broadly today. When he left Shinnoah, never had he expected to work glashiin again. But now that the opportunity was upon him, he couldn't wait to get started. He'd extend his countertop into a workbench. It shouldn't be too hard. He'd also need a small forge for melting the glashiin down. Stamps and pressers, he could make with wood, if he could find the right sort.

"Alright, I'll trust your word and await this special, mysterious, <u>something</u> you are planning. Knowing you, though it may be strange, it will also have a measure of the wonderful."

"Sometimes you say the nicest things, my friend," Outh'n beamed.

"Un'yel," she corrected with a shake of her head.

"What? Is that 'friend' in Genzetti tongue?"

She shook her head again, her carefully arranged curls holding fast. The glashiin beads glittered happily within the twisted strands. "No. It is the term for an older female sibling who is not bloodkyn." She frowned.

"You mean, you wish to be my older sadau?"

She shook her head. "No, I mean, I view you as my ki'im anyil and I didn't even realize it until now."

"So, younger male sibling?"

She nodded and raised an eyebrow, as if daring him to refute her words.

He shrugged. "I'm happy to be thought of in such a way. I left a favored sadau behind me in Shinnoah and it would be good to have family again." The words brought back his precipitous departure and the wall that separated him from his blood relations. He frowned as his mood dampened.

"Cheer up, Outh'n," Eiva encouraged. "You may never see her again here, but as long as she is following the path of Andurdrao, you will see her when you meet in the life beyond, eiya?"

Outh'n nodded, but held any words back. They wouldn't be so nice if he set them free right now. Besides, he knew she meant well.

"So, what now? You've gotten your hair done. It's certainly awe-inspiring. The glashiin beads catch the light in just the right way." He paused as he cast a critical eye over his friend. "You highlighted your eyes, too, eiya?" When she nodded and smiled, he went on. "Who did you see? They certainly did it well. It looks natural but also other-worldly."

"My thanks, Outh'n," Eiva preened. "What about the clothing?"

Outh'n grinned as she avoided his question about where she had it all done. He honestly didn't know a single male she wouldn't impress with her efforts. Eiva was already lovely on the outside. The clothing she'd chosen today accented every curve and revealed much more than a Shinnoahn maid would consider proper. But he'd seen other Genzetti females on Yacan. This seemed to be something they usually did. Eiva always pushed the boundaries, though. If he was her target, he'd probably have mixed feelings. He decided on honesty.

"Look, I," Outh'n began, took a breath and as her face darkened, rushed on, "I'm Shinnoahn. If I saw my potential life-mate wearing even the more modest clothes Genzetti females seem to prefer, I'd want to lock her in a room where no one else could see her. But that doesn't mean you don't look amazing. If Kol doesn't agree, he needs a new set of eyes worse than I do."

At that, she punched his shoulder in glee. "You had me so worried, ki'im anyil! I was ready to rip your throat out with my bare hands." She was laughing, but Outh'n knew that wasn't an idle jest. She'd done such a thing before. He'd been a witness to the hapless intruder's death.

"Alright. I think I'm ready. Will you wish me well?"

Outh'n thought for a moment before remembering the Genzetti parting phrase. "Walk well the path, Un'yel."

She didn't walk. She sped down the path, her bags no hindrance in her haste to meet with Kol.

A THUMP AGAINST HIS door roused Outh'n from his deep thoughts. Since he'd watched Eiva disappear down the path, he'd been trying to figure out how to set up a place in his cabin for his work, now that he had a glashiin supplier. His chair creaked as he rose to open his door. Eiva sat slumped against the frame. He knelt so quickly, he bruised his knees. She was in awful shape, though. His knees would heal.

"Eiva," he called as he gently shook her shoulder. Genzetti didn't touch others and he really shouldn't touch her either. But how did one determine the health of another without touching them when they wouldn't respond verbally? "Eiva? Can you hear me?"

She rolled her head upward, still leaning on his door framed. "You're messing up your beautiful hair," he gently cautioned.

"It doesn't matter." She gestured weakly to all the new things they'd worked so hard to gather earlier. "None of these matters."

"Why?" Outh'n figured he knew, but he asked anyway. Sometimes, it was better to sear the wound rather than risk infection.

"He doesn't want me." The tiny confession was so unlike his larger-than-life, overly confident friend. He wasn't sure how to help her. So he waited. "He said he's not looking for a life-mate." She barked a mirthless chuckle and added. "It's a lie, of course. Every Genzetti male is looking for a life-mate who will bring them good connections."

"Maybe he's just not ready yet," Outh'n offered weakly. Kol was determination incarnate, though Outh'n thought the man was more determined to be awkward. There were some dawnings Outh'n wondered if Kol tried to make everyone else feel like they were less committed than he was.

Eiva rolled her head from side to side. "He says never."

"Come in for kafkhet and we can talk more," Outh'n gently urged. He thought she might refuse, but after several heartbeats, she nodded once and rose slowly to her full height.

"Thank you for the offer. I could use a cup of something warm since it seems my target leaves my arms bereft."

Outh'n turned so she couldn't see the grin that refused to behave itself. He headed straight for his counter and small cooking area. "Sit anywhere you feel comfortable. I don't know if my furniture works for Genzetti comfort, but you're welcome to try."

"Thank you ki'im anyil."

When the kafkhet was done and they each held a steaming beaker, Outh'n asked, "What will you do now?"

"What do life-mate do when the one they love won't look at them?" She murmured, then breathed deep the scent of the rich kafkhet.

"Keep trying," Outh'n answered without thought.

Eiva's eyes flicked open, spearing him with a razor sharp gaze over the rim of her cup. They glittered more than her beads as a smile broadened her features. She cocked her head to the side, one eyebrow lifted, and murmured, "I will take your advice, Outh'n Durr. I feel much better already. Thank you," she intoned. She set her cup on the table between them and something creaked. It grew louder, and both of them scanned the room for the cause when suddenly, Eiva shrieked.

The chair she'd chosen had spindle legs and one of them had broken. She lay sprawled on one side next to the collapsed chair, her shoulders shaking. Outh'n couldn't tell if it was fury or merriment, and he wasn't about to guess.

A toss of her hair and a bark of laughter assured him all was well. He quickly offered his help as they both laughed over the incident. How he'd fix the chair, he didn't know, but he'd get it done. It was worth it to see his best friend smiling again.

22 Celebration

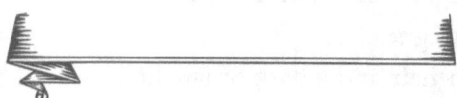

"Outh'n Durr," the call sounded far behind him. Outh'n paused on the suspended rope bridge leading to the second sparring platform. He turned as Kol bounded up to him. He set his feet firmly on the wooden plank and rode the waves without grabbing for the ropes on either side of him. It had taken him longer than some to get used to the motion.

"What's got you all excited, iteik'I?"

"You aren't my eik'it after your win yesterday." Kol grinned.

"Are you... is that..." he stuttered in disbelief. Finally, he clamped his lips together and nodded.

"Hey, I thought you'd rejoice. What's this?" Kol grumbled. "I thought we could go to the tak'kobi."

"Tak'kobi?"

Kol pointed to the many piercings adorning his ears, brows, and nose, and Outh'n's blood ran cold. "No thanks, Kol. I don't mind getting injured while I'm working, but poking holes in my skin on purpose?" He shook his head slowly.

"Are you certain? It's a mark of honor in Genzetti society."

"But this isn't Genzet. And, if my skin color didn't give it away already, I'm Shinnoahn."

Kol chuckled and Outh'n marveled at the difference it made to his appearance. "Well, what do Shinnoahns do to mark a victorious finish?"

Outh'n thought for a while and said, "Enjoy a celebration with friends," then tacked on, "I guess."

"You guess?" Kol's brow wrinkled. "Have you never marked a personal victory, Outh'n Durr?"

Outh'n shrugged. "I won a big tournament in my village once."

Kol waited for more, but he wouldn't be hearing it from Outh'n's mouth. Not unless the actual voice of of Tugansol demanded it of him.

"I take it there was no celebration with friends for this win."

Outh'n kept silent and walked on down the path.

"I offer my apologies, Outh'n."

"For what?" Outh'n worked hard to keep his voice neutral, but a cracked growl probably gave everything away to the observant Genzetti.

"Bringing up terrible memories?" Kol answered uncertainly.

"You didn't. I was very proud of my hard work and the achievement. My family was also proud."

Kol nodded. "Then, when the suns set, let's meet at the Byrnir and have that celebration, eh?"

"I'm bringing Eiva." Outh'n threw down the challenge boldly.

"You should," he answered without rancor. "She is your friend."

"Un'yel, she says."

Kol's eyebrows shot up. "Did she? She claims you as im anyil?"

"Ki'im anyil," he clarified.

Kol roared with laughter. The deep sound of his merriment echoed through the forest and startled a group of nesting flyers.

"If you weren't laughing at me, I'd say you should laugh more." Outh'n grumbled.

"I'm not laughing at you, but at her. That's such an interesting twist. Something I didn't expect from her."

"Why'd you reject her?"

Kol's mirth disappeared completely. "How did you know about that?" he growled.

Outh'n shrugged. "I'm her friend. She asked me for help."

"Help with what?" The growl no longer disturbed Outh'n, but he did tense himself, ready for battle if the bigger man's temper got the better of him.

"She asked for my opinion when she went shopping." When Kol said nothing, he added, "She didn't really need anything from me except approval, though I doubt she'd have taken me seriously had I disagreed with any of her purchases."

They'd crossed the second platform and were heading onto the rope bridge on the far side, which led farther up to the third and highest platform. Kol stopped and Outh'n turned to face him when he realized.

"What's wrong with that, Kol?"

"What's wrong?" He shook his head as if coming out of a daze. "She worked that hard, eiya?"

Outh'n nodded. "She did. I've never seen her smile so brightly."

"I am sorry, Outh'n Durr. Truly I am. I have no intention of taking a life-mate at this point."

"She told me as much when she saw me again."

Maybe Outh'n's face gave away more than he thought it did because Kol asked, "What did you tell her?"

"She asked me what Shinnoahns did when the one they loved rejected them." These questions were getting uncomfortable.

"And?" He really didn't want to answer that question. He could feel the bruises forming already, but the man deserved an answer. And maybe, in all this, he might help his friend.

"I answered her truthfully. Because she's my friend."

"What did you tell her, Outh'n Durr?" He'd grown so used to Kol's annoyed growl and the clipped syllables, it had little effect on him now. Still, he prepared himself. He might not know Kol well, but he knew the man wouldn't like his reply.

"Shinnoahns keep trying."

Kol swung at him, but Outh'n ducked. A suspension bridge was not really the place for a scuffle, but he hadn't chosen it. Remembering there was water beneath this one, Outh'n took a risk and dove off the bridge rather than give Kol the satisfaction of pounding him into a bruised mess. Right before he cut through the surface of the water, Outh'n wondered whether the celebration would still take place.

EIVA HAD OUTDONE HERSELF. She glittered from head to toe with glashiin beads in her hair, which she'd worn down in waves, and her fitted silver-gray dress sparkled with more of the little baubles. Even though her dress showed every curve, she'd taken Outh'n's advice and covered most of her skin. A single slit on one side hinted at the Eiva Di'Amo people usually saw. More baubles dotted her brow bone, accenting her piercings there. Her sharpened, painted fingernails shimmered night-sky-dome blue and matched some of the beads. The color covering her eyelids matched her dress and nails, and a thick black line outlined each. Somehow, it made the rich violet of her eyes stand out. Outh'n whistled in appreciation.

"You look amazing, Un'yel." He looked down at his own attire, which was modest by comparison. Wide-legged breeches gathered at the hem nestled into the cuffs of his best brown hide boots. He liked the flap, which was embossed with a simple border pattern of interlocking squares. He had topped the dark green breeches with a flame red tunic. The deep 'v' neckline bore a simple brown cord for lacing. A black vest embroidered with a simple green vine at the edges complete the ensemble. Colorful, yes, but much less so than what he might've worn back home.

"I feel under-dressed beside you." He offered her a wry grin.

Eiva's merriment was infectious. "Come on, Outh'n. We both have much to celebrate."

When they'd walked down the path a while, Eiva said, "I hear there's a tournament coming soon."

"A tournament? What kind of tournament?" Outh'n enjoyed games of skill as long as death wasn't a possible result. He hoped this was such a tournament.

"There are rumors the Ammir is not in good health. A new one has to take her place."

"Ammir?" Outh'n choked on the word. "They're choosing a new one?"

"Yes, Outh'n. Are you paying attention at all?" Eiva's exasperation was palpable. "If you're going to be like this all dusking, I might just leave you on your own."

"I guess you have to do what you feel is right, Eiva." Outh'n wouldn't give her the satisfaction of knowing how much that hurt. She'd already adjusted to the news. There was high honor awarded to her family name. He'd had to work hard to gain any honor at all, while the rest of his family had the respect of his village.

"There's somewhere we need to stop first." Eiva could barely contain her excitement. Who knew what she was planning now?

"Alright," he grumbled.

Eiva chuckled. "I was teasing earlier. I wouldn't leave you on your own, not on this dusking. This party is for those who have successfully completed their training, those who will formally join the Myrr. Why would I leave my ki'im anyil who is equal to me in rank because he has worked hard, just like me?"

Outh'n shook his head. "So, where are we going?"

"You'll see."

"Eiva," Outh'n began, but stopped when they reached a hide-worker's shop. "What are we doing here?"

"Come on," Eiva smiled and beckoned him into the store.

"But it's surely closed for the celebration." Outh'n wasn't sure why, but he suddenly feared going in. Eiva wore her mischievous smile, and he wasn't sure he wanted to be part of the joke.

She gave him no option, grabbing him by the elbow and dragging him in. "Thank you for keeping the shop open a little longer," she greeted the shop-keep. "Do you have the item I ordered?"

"It's ready," the dour man behind the counter nodded and pulled a wrapped parcel out from under his table.

Eiva passed over the payment, and the dour expression dissolved into joyous thanks. How much had she paid for this? Eiva handed him the package. "Here. Congratulations, ki'im anyil."

Outh'n stared at the brown wrapped parcel, then at Eiva, then back at the parcel. She shook it, then pressed it into his hand when he refused to reach for it. "You deserve it, Outh'n. You have been a great encouragement to me."

Outh'n pulled at the string. "But I don't have anything for you." His protest was weak. When was the last time someone had given him a gift?

The paper fell away, revealing a beautifully embossed, buttery soft bix'n hide eye patch. A leafy vine decorated the outer edge of the eyepiece. A spear and shield adorned the eyepiece. The interlocking square border which decorated his boots, ran the length of the strap. Tears threatened, but he held them back.

"Do you have a mirror, shop-keep?" he murmured as he studied the strap and the buckle.

"We do. Please. Look here." The small mirror on the table was adequate for Outh'n to don the eye patch and check the fit. After a couple of minor changes, his hair hung just right and the eye patch fit comfortably against his skin.

He turned to Eiva. "I know it's not done, but I'm hugging you, Eiva Di'Amo."

And he wrapped his arms around the surprised woman. After a moment, she hugged him awkwardly back.

"Now, come on," she urged. "We have a celebration to attend."

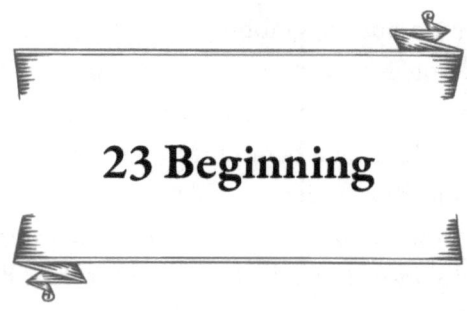

23 Beginning

The air was heavy, hardly breathable. Well, at least, Outh'n struggled. It didn't look like Kol was having the same issue. Or any issue. Anger flowed hot, fast, and acidic through Outh'n's veins. He did his best to tamp it down, but all he saw was a giant of a man who didn't even have to break a sweat before Outh'n was almost out of the fight completely.

"Get up, Outh'n," Kol taunted. "Surely that's not all you've got."

"You Genzetti—" The swing of Kol's staff cut off his words. Had Outh'n been any slower in rolling to the side, he'd have lost the final round right then.

At the celebration the previous night, the Ammir had officially announced her time was ending. She called out a list of names and told them to prepare for the tournament today. Outh'n wasn't the only one surprised to hear his name called. Eiva was also on the list and, if possible, she was more surprised than he was. She'd fought her battles with the single-minded fury of a Di'shi dervish, but Keila, an Ikhel'duri woman by birth, had bested her in the end.

Outh'n had made it to the final round, surprising himself. But Kol would be hard to beat and he wasn't even sure he wanted the position. His own people had banished him from home, and he wasn't able to save his best friend's life. If he couldn't take care of his own family and friend, how could he care for the many who lived on Yacan?

The whistle and thwack of Kol's staff singed his eardrums. How did he put so much behind his blows? He was big, a walking bag of muscle, but surely there was more to it. Now was not the time to study, though. He should've paid closer attention during the training sessions.

He dodged to the left, only to realize Kol had feinted, as the staff circled back to catch him a winding blow in the ribs. He shifted to wuveia form, thinking he would be better off armored with a sturdier and more agile body.

Kol also shifted after tossing the staff to the platform floor. Then they paced, sizing each other up. The two were more evenly matched in their vesat'ya forms, though their body structures differed. The older man had explained a little about the karyna, how they hunted, how they killed, and a little about their environment.

From Oowah, he'd learned how wuveia were stealthy hunters. He also remembered his friend was extremely patient. He'd been able to practice using these tools in his wuveia arsenal. But whether this form was powerful enough to best Kol's was another matter entirely. He'd been quick enough to defeat Eiva's last opponent, though that woman had defeated his friend. Adept at changing his skin, he was not — at least, not as good as he thought he should be. Tugansol had all the credit for saving his skin during his last skirmish. Keila should have won.

Kol's sleek tail twitched and Outh'n readied himself to dodge, looking for any sign of which direction to move.

The big black karyna moved like wind through grass-covered mountain meadows. The motion sent the rays of the suns skittering over Kol's glossy fur as he readied himself to pounce.

Outh'n tried to anticipate the exact moment he'd need to dodge, but Kol was careful. All but Outh'n's left flank escaped unscathed. A deep, searing gash appeared where one of Kol's claws had ripped through the flesh. Though in severe pain, Outh'n struggled to stand on his paws. He managed, but only just. And by the time he had, Kol stood over him, saying nothing, simply looking on and waiting to see what Outh'n would do.

He could try for Kol's throat. A faint snarl escaped as his lips curled away to reveal his sharp teeth.

"I wouldn't," Kol's voice was quiet, but firm. Outh'n wasn't sure what rankled more — the fact that a karyna bested a wuveia, or that his every move had been predictable. Maybe it was that Kol's tone which held no contempt for his pitiful efforts.

In the end, he acknowledged he was no match for Kol. He bowed, his nose almost touching the ground, admitting defeat and ignoring the knot of disappointment in his belly. Then he limped to the edge of the platform and sat gingerly to avoid further pain in his leg.

Once Serafin announced the winner and the Ammir led Kol away, the survivors limped away from the arena. Eiva joined Outh'n as he trudged back to his cabin.

"You did well today, Outh'n," she purred in that velvety voice. He snorted in derision, not bothering to reply. "Well, I thought you did. It seems you disagree."

Outh'n sighed. Her tone showed him she wouldn't let this go. "No. I did everything I thought I could to win."

"Then you did well," she insisted. "My old iteik'i once told me all we can do is our best. To attempt anything beyond our best is impossible and will often result in a needless death or injury on the battlefield."

Outh'n couldn't help but grin at how old-fashioned the words sounded to his ears. His teachers had often spoken that way. "Really?" he asked. "What else did this teacher say?"

"He told me I would do well on the battlefield because I was so good at strategy and quick of wit." She beamed, baring her fangs. The sparkle of pride in her eyes warmed Outh'n's chilled heart a little. At least he was not alone in losing and he still had a friend.

"I still can't get past my win over your opponent, Eiva. How could she have missed that opening? My ribs were completely exposed. And long enough to have gotten in a killing blow. Why did she hesitate?"

Eiva shrugged. "Who knows? Maybe she was worried she really would kill you." She shrugged again so smoothly, it reminded Outh'n of Kol's rippling fur-covered muscles before he pounced for the last time. He shivered instinctively.

"But I thought that was to be expected in such a match," he spoke to clear his mind of the image more than anything else. "They warned us."

The purple braids bobbed and swung as his friend nodded. "Indeed. In sparring, there's always the chance someone won't dodge fast enough or will trip and fall off the platform."

"How can you discuss these lost lives so coldly? They were our fellows, Eiva," Outh'n chided.

"Not mine. Kol is, yes. There are a few others like yourself I find amusing or interesting." She waved her manicured fingers in front of her as if to shoo away stinging insects. "But most of the warriors living here barely deserve the name. If they can't keep up, they're only hindering the rest of us." She stopped, gripping Outh'n's elbow to halt his progress. He turned to face her. "Make no mistake, Outh'n. You have a gift. If you weren't special, I wouldn't be here and you wouldn't be calling me by any name at all if you wished to keep your tongue attached."

Outh'n cocked his head to one side. "Are you serious?" At her crisp nod, he asked, "Why?"

"Why what?"

"Why bother with me? You've already seen I'm not good enough to best Kol."

She snickered at that. The snicker grew into a rich and glorious belly laugh. When she'd calmed enough, she gasped out, "Outh'n, no one in this place can best Kol." She shook her head. "Have you really not heard the tales of Shadow and Storm?"

He shook his head, so she continued. "There is no time, and the stories are from a faraway place, but know this. Those names hold weight even now in my home. Shadow and Storm were an unbeatable duo for many tsimikin until one man brought them down with treachery. Everyone says he was their friend at the time. Because of this one man, exile and separation of two friends resulted. Guardian Bal Shif reassigned them, sent them away from the tasks and people they loved most."

"Betrayal by fellow villagers is tough. I could imaging a friend's betrayal being worse. They have my sympathy."

"Are you certain?" At his nod, she continued. "One of them is here. You could speak to him and give him your condolences."

Outh'n stared up at her for a long while. He couldn't tell what it was, but she wasn't telling him everything.

"Who is he, Eiva?" he groused.

"I think you already know, Outh'n Durr." His tone irked her. He didn't care. She didn't tease unless there was some kind of morbid pleasure to be gained from it. And he didn't appreciate her using that tactic on him.

Then he realized. "Kol is Shadow," he stated dully. When she nodded once, he said, "I fought the great and mighty Shadow and lived, then. That's what you're trying to tell me. That's why you say I did well."

She nodded again. "As I said, Outh'n Durr, there is something special about you. I will continue my friendship with you."

They turned to walk down the path in silence, Outh'n lost in his own thoughts. So Kol not only training in battle before arriving, he was in battle-tried as well. How had any of that tournament been fair? Why didn't the Ammir just hand-pick him?

Unless he asked the Ammir or Edrea, he would probably never know. But from this point on, Outh'n Durr would do his best to match up to Kol Udota in every way. What adventure awaited him on that trail?

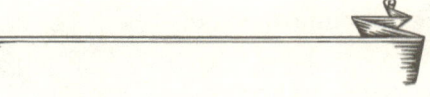

Glossary

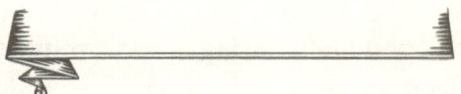

• Abei - son (Shinnoah)

• Arb'la - a sleek, four-footed herd animal used strictly as mounts by the Shinnoahn people. Messengers prefer them because they are swift and sure-footed.

• Babei - (formal) father (Shinnoah)

• Babeiya - (informal) poppa or dad (Shinnoah)

• Bah'riim - bear-like creatures with sharp teeth and claws, predatory mammals which eat only meat, have sharp eyesight and hearing, and are not really interested in humans if smaller, easier prey is near.

• Bizhal - fluffy, small mammal of Shinnoah, friendly, insectivorous, slightly telepathic

• Daula - daughter (Shinnoah)

• D'kine - a domesticated biped, something like a furry reptile in its nature, used as a mount by Shinnoahn farmers.

• Hesp - a hand-span, used to measure length in approximations, whether that means someone's height or the hours of a day.

- Insia - largest Shinnoahn coin

- Iyaba - brother (Shinnoah)

- Kaila - jail, holding cell

- Kinzhik - poisonous, flying insect whose thin wings reflecting light in an aurora, coveted for unique artisan crafts. One sting can make a full-grown man ill for days, or even kill an already unhealthy man.

- Kre'li - an under-dweller of the forest floor of Yacan. Mud and muck is its home and much about this creature remains a mystery. All one ever sees is the mesmerizing pair of claws it uses to capture its prey.

- Miklanin - a shrub whose leaves and miniscule pale pink blossoms emit a light, sweet fragrance on the bush, but when crushed, the scent is extremely overwhelming and foul.

- Moyri - mother (Shinnoah)

- Raug'l - a croaking, insect-like creature having two sets of wings and eight legs.

- Sadau - sister (Shinnoah)

- Sepi - a sticky substance used like sealing wax on messages, comes from an evergreen of Shinnoah and northern M'Neshunnaya

- Shinma - smallest Shinnoahn coin

- Silti - a snakelike relative of the slitchit of M'Neshunnaya, it carries poison in a barb on its tail.

- Surteit - Dark Realm (Shinnoah)

- Tiav'yag - wanderer, traitor to Shinnoah

- Tugansol - Life Giver - Shinnoahn name for Creator Deity

- Whe'evet - Across between a wolf and an ox having shaggy, ropy, mottled gray fur; long, elegant muzzles; cloven ears; sharp, curved fangs; dinner-plate-sized paws; a single short curving horn growing between their ears; three sets of red eyes sometimes hidden in their shaggy fur; can only see in infrared; travel in packs; move silently; native to northern mountains of Shinnoah; known as vicious predators

- Wuve - the smaller domesticated cousins of the wuveia who roam the forests of Shinnoah in packs.

- Wuveia - wolf-like creatures which are solitary hunters but live in small packs during breeding season. Long snouts, muscular build, broader at the shoulders, narrower at the hips, with longer tails and broader foot pads tipped with claws to navigate easily through narrow twists and turns.

- Yuenda - teacher (Shinnoah)

- Zoleta - Golden Realm (Shinnoah)

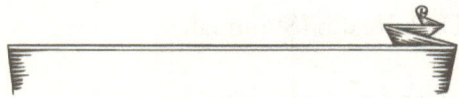

Index
Time Flow On Y'Dahnndrya

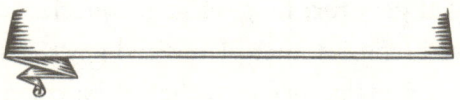

There are 684 days in a Y'Dahnndryan year. A year is called a tsimik, or tsimikin when plural, named for the sister suns, Tsifi'ra and Mit'ra. There are six seasons, or dahlsikin, in each year. One season is a dahlsik, marked by the passing of the smallest moon, Dahl. Each dahlsik includes three minsikin, or months. Min is the largest moon and marks the minsikin. Each minsik contains four nine-day weeks. The word <u>nainda</u> refers to one or more weeks. A day is most often referred to as a <u>dawning</u> and a night is sometimes referred to as a <u>dusking</u>.

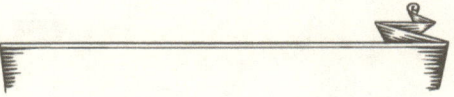

List of the Dahlsikin and Their Minsikin

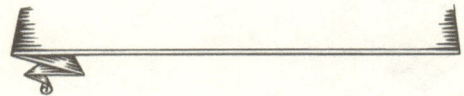

Ik'shi - Season of Storms - harsh/cool - The stormy months are Koziki, Domiki, and Grokiki.

Y'ma- Season of Planting - mild/warm - The planting months are Yarma, Memma, and Hanma.

Ek'shi - Season of Rains - mild/warming to hot - The rainy months are Zazinek, Fezek, and Shizek.

Y'aam - Season of Harvest - mild but drying/ hot to warm - The harvest months are Yannat, Yappat, and Yarrom.

Di'shi - Season of Wind - dry/cool - The windy seasons are Nondi, Ragadi, and Maradi.

Ni'shi - Season of Ice - harsh/cold - The icy months are Shiini, Iriini, and Glokni.

Dawnings of the Nainda

K oz, Mem, Ara, Zet, Mut, Za, Ki, Irsh, and Gok are the commonly used names for each day of the nainda.

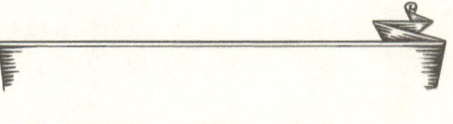

About The Clans

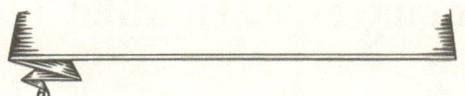

Y'Dahnndrya hosts six clans. Three of them have territory on the Eastern continent, Sheromoth. These are Shinnoah in the north, D'Koruyi in the south-west, and M'Neshunnaya in the south-east. Two are on the western continent, Emidar. The clans on this continent are Genzet in the north and Bot'ha in the south. The last clan, Ik'heldur, includes all the islands of Y'Dahnndrya.

The Three Clans of Sheromoth, Their Languages, & Familial Titles

M'Neshunnayan Clan - Language: Shunya (SHOON ya) - Father: Fatir (FAH teer); Mother: Matir (MAH teer); Grandfather: Zat'Fatir (ZAHT fah teer); Grandmother: Zat'Matir (ZAHT mah teer); Daughter: Datir (DAH teer); Son: Shoneh (SHOW neh); Sister: Siveh (SEE veh); Brother: Batir (BAH teer); Aunt: Tani (TAH nee)

D'Koruyin Clan - Language: Koryu (KOR yoo) - Father: Pareh (PAH reh); Mother: Morah (MORE ah); Daughter: Oori (OH ree); Son: Azho (AH zho); Sister: Mireti (mee RET ee); Brother: Bramet (BRAH met)

Shinnoahn Clan - Language: Oahn (OH ahn) - Father: Babei - formal (bah BAY) or Babeiya - informal (bah BAY yah); Mother: Moyri (MOYi ree); Daughter: Daula (DOW lah); Son: Abei (AH bay); Sister: Sadau (sah DOW); Brother: Iyaba (ee YAH bah)

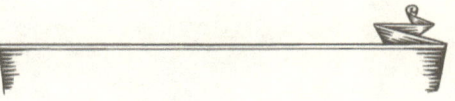

The Two Clans of Emidar, Their Languages, & Familial Titles

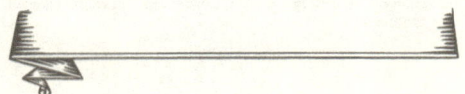

Genzet Clan - Language: Enzi (EHN zee) - Father: A'ada (AH' AH dah); Mother: imi'I (ee MEE' ee); Son: O'oso (OH' OH soh); Daughter: ulu'U (oo LOO' oo); Brother: O'boer (OH' boh AIR); Sister: luer'U (loo AIR' oo); honorary little brother: Ki'im Anyil (kee EEM an YEEL); honorary big sister: un'Yel (oon YELL)

Bot'ha Clan - Language: Othwa (OHTH wah) - Father: Padri (PAH dree); Mother: Madri (MAH dree); Daughter: Lenal (leh NAHL); Son: Fari (FAH ree); Sister: Eisys (AIS yis); Brother: Fibyr (feeb YIR)

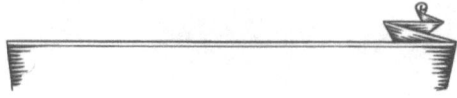

The Clan of the Islands

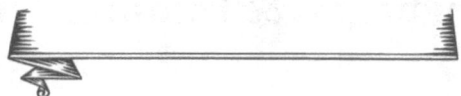

I khel'dur Clan - Language: Keldu (KEL doo) - Father: Peliir (peh LEEER); Mother: Amarin (ah mah REEN); Daughter: Arini (ah REE nee); Son: Eliir (eh LEER); Sister: Bemin (BEH meen); Brother: Fimir (FEE meer)

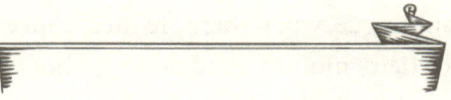

Pronunciation Guide & Other Helpful Information

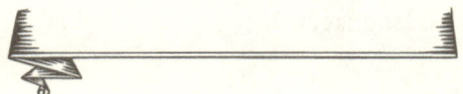

1. Y'Dahnndrya - pronounced (yi DAHN dree ya) - think of the initial 'Y' as you would in the name Yvonne or Yvette in which the ending of the syllable is clipped.
2. M'Neshunnaya - Pronounce both the 'M' and the 'N' but together (mNEH shuh NIGH uh)
3. D'Koruyi - Pronounce the 'D' and the 'K' together so that the 'd' is clipped (dKOR oo yee)
4. Shinnoah - (shee NOH ah)
5. Genzet - (GEHN zeht)
6. Bot'ha - (BOAT hah)
7. Ikhel'dur - The 'h' is a slight breath in the second syllable and the third syllable having the sound of the oo of moon. (EEK hel door)
8. Y'Dahnndrya has two suns, Tsifi'ra (the greater) and Mit'ra (the lesser). (TSEE fee rah) and (MEET rah)
9. Y'Dahnndrya has five moons. Min (MEEN) and Dahl (as expected by spelling) are called the Guide Moons since their paths can be counted on to mark seasons and months. The calendar was created with their help. The other moons are Go'it (GOH iht), Yur'e (YOOR eh), and Shoth'a (SHOWTH ah), the last with a voiced th as in 'then'.
10. Though each clan has its own tongue, and some have a secret warrior language, all the clans speak Genra (GEHN rah), the

common tongue, when there are inter-clan events.

11. Since the deity most focused on in my books up to date is a creator god, I searched for words in various languages that fit the description. Each clan calls this deity by a different name, but they all mean 'Creator' in some way. I simply chose a pronunciation that worked with the other words I'd created in the clan languages.

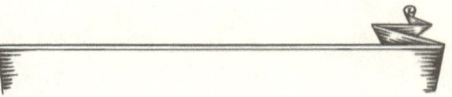

Clan - Name of the Creator and Pronunciation - Meaning

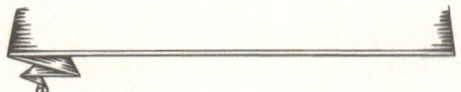

S hinnoahn Clan - Tugansol (TOO gahn sohl) - Life Giver
     M'Neshunnayan Clan - Azilet'zal (ah ZEE let zahl) - Thread of Life

D'Koruyin Clan - Kai'yanga (keye' YAHN gah) - Creator

Ikhel'dur Clan - Kwikrei'ya (kwee KRAY' yah) - One Who Creates

Bot'ha Clan - Changjo'ja (chahng JO jah) - Creator

Genzet Clan - Andurdrao (ahn DOOR drow) - Breath of Life

When Reading Names of People, Places and Unfamiliar Things:

- A's most often say 'ah'.

- E's most often say 'eh'.

- I's most often say 'ee'.

- O's most often say 'oh'.

- U's most often say 'oo' like 'moon'.

- When vowels are combined (like - 'oa' or 'ai' or 'ei') simply combine the above sounds.

- Doubled letters denote a slightly elongated sound, such as 'ii' = 'ee' + 'ee'.

- R's are slightly rolled, unless doubled when the rolling is more pronounced.

- G's are always hard, as in 'garden'.

- TH's are always voiced, such as in the word 'then'.

- Apostrophes denote a clip or short break between syllables, not necessarily an accent on the preceding syllable.

For example: Sari'i would be pronounced "sah REE ee" and Kai'yanga is pronounced (kai YAHN gah).

• Otherwise, if a name or word looks familiar, use a familiar pronunciation. I'm not picky about how you say the names of anything in my book world. Have fun with it!

Author's Note

T hank you so much for reading my first novella and my second published work of literature. You are awesome and you bring a smile to my face.

The Tale of Outh'n Durr was a difficult project to complete. Outh'n is a complex character for me and his story was almost as odd as I attempted to put it into words. As such, I know it took me far too long to get everything together, at least in the minds of the readers who've enjoyed Ripples (Children of Y'Dahnndrya book 1)[1]. My apologies to you, dear Readers! I have to work when I'm able and as the ideas come to me. Editing a book is also a time-consuming task. Add to that, I have no desire to put a book out which I can't enjoy reading myself. Outh'n's tale, I feel confident, is as done as can be. Now I can move on to refining book two, Surge, as well as the three other novels in the series (so far) and the five shorter stories, like Outh'n's, which fill out info on a few more side characters, as well as the mythos of Y'Dahnndrya.

I couldn't have done any of this if it hadn't been for my super-supportive family and friends: John, Noah, Judy, Randy, Shiloh, Rowan, Ruth, Robert, Christina, Brenda, Jay, Julie, Russ, Matt, Danny, Danny 2.0, the Alliance of Independent Authors[2], and of course, the creators and mods of NaNoWriMo.

You may or may not know, I also create the covers for my books. Normally, I guess this stuff would show up in the front of the book.

1.   http://books2read.com/RipplesCoD1

2.   http://www.allianceindependentauthors.org

Still, I want to make sure the information is accessible for the creators to get the credit due them. These awesome photographers and digital artists who offered their work as open source elements on Pixabay deserve a shout-out.

- The Forest Background - Image by Darkmoon Art from Pixabay[3]

- The Background Bokeh Overlay - Image by AStoko from Pixabay[4]

- The Background Aurora Overlay - Image by AStoko from Pixabay[5]

- The Frame - Image by Annalise Batista from Pixabay[6]

- The Blue Jeweltone Corner Accents - Image by MR1313 from Pixabay[7]

- The Leather Frame Background - Image by Binho Bianchi from Pixabay[8]

- The Art Deco Title, Author, and Blurb Border Element - Image by Annalise Batista from Pixabay[9]

- The Fire-wolf Cover Image - I originally downloaded this element from a website which is now defunct. I think the

---

3. http://pixabay.com/photos/forest-wilderness-fantasy-trees-3877365/

4. http://pixabay.com/illustrations/bokeh-violet-purple-background-4542479/

5. http://pixabay.com/illustrations/light-to-dye-snow-heaven-aurora-4537085/

6. http://pixabay.com/illustrations/gold-foil-art-deco-frame-frame-5816239/

7. http://pixabay.com/illustrations/sample-element-injection-frame-4254643/

8. http://pixabay.com/photos/leather-texture-wallpaper-1222379/

9. http://pixabay.com/illustrations/gold-foil-dividers-divider-frame-5920961/

site was called Clipart123 or something like that. Even so, I believe the creator didn't leave a name to mention. Still, I would like to thank the unknown creator for sharing this awesome image which matches my story so well.

• The Stained Glass Purple, White, Green, and Pink elements are my own digital artwork.

There's one Person I could do nothing without, and that's my Savior, the Messiah Yeshua. Yes, my religious beliefs shape who I am and how I conduct myself. Yes, those beliefs affect my writing to a certain extent. My prayer is that every person who picks up this book will be able to enjoy it and gain something positive from the reading of it. I'm praying for each one of you. My statement of faith follows for those wishing to know more about my beliefs.

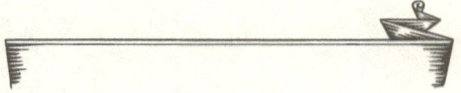

More About the Author
Introduction

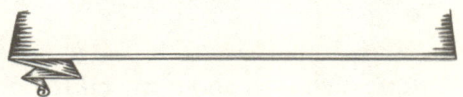

I t took me quite a while to determine whether or not I should actually put this out there. Some folks are quite adamant about not reading books by Christian authors, no matter if they are preachy or not. However, I think there are some readers who'd like to know more about me, what I believe, and why I believe the way I do. This is for those readers.

My History

One reason I don't say much about my faith journey is because I feel like there are few who can relate. I was raised in a relatively happy home, supplied with all I needed to grow properly, achieve goals, and thrive. My parents have always been together and I have never doubted their love for me. We weren't rich, but we had what we needed and it took me a while to understand that, to understand that what a person needs often differs greatly from what they think they need. I often bemoaned the fact that I didn't wear the same clothes as the cool kids or have the same kinds of toys or gadgets. My dad was a farmer on a small farm. As such, there was never really enough money for those upper middle class items and certainly none for luxury items. We didn't even have a Nintendo until I was well into my teenage years, and we got that one used and only had two games for it. Still, I knew I was loved. I knew I had a warm bed to sleep in and good, sturdy clothes to wear. I never went to bed hungry. And I occasionally got to have special treats, usually a favorite snack or something equally inexpensive.

Another thing I grew up with was music. Music is my first true passion. I love to sing and will take every opportunity to do so. I especially love to sing with my family or anyone who can sing harmony and improvise. I can play the piano, mostly like Elizabeth Bennet, "...a little and very poorly, I'm afraid." I can also play the guitar in a similar fashion. But singing, ah! I wish I'd been able to do something with that earlier on in my life. I considered majoring in it in college but my mom talked me out of it. It's probably a good thing. I didn't like opera until much later in life and if they'd made me sing such things in college, I'd likely be biased against it now. Music is a huge part of my family life. Most of my family sings and we usually sing when we get together.

One place music really came alive for me was in church. I was in church from day one. My mother has been playing the piano in church since she was twelve and my dad was the worship leader for years before PTSD pulled him away from it. They were part of a traveling gospel music quartet and we visited churches all over southern Louisiana during the younger years of my life and until I was into my teen years. Their music used to be on YouTube, but I can't find it anymore. I used to sing in the middle of their performances to give them a break. I loved it!

Then I became a teen and it was just "old hat." I wanted to sing more contemporary songs which didn't really fit in with southern and country gospel. I also lost focus for a while. But I'm getting ahead of myself.

Hearing God's Call

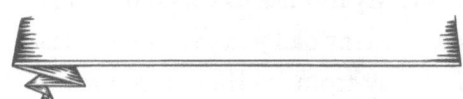

At a summer evening service in a small Southern Baptist country church, the sun shone gold through the westward-facing, rectangular, colored glass panes of the church windows. The air conditioning was working hard to keep up with the southern Louisiana heat and humidity. I was sitting with friends of my family, I think, listening to the sermon. At the end, when the pastor gave the altar call, he asked if there was anyone who wanted to be saved, encouraged them to step forward, and asked them to come pray with him. I surprised everyone, I think, but I stepped up and prayed that prayer.

"Dear Lord,

I know I'm a sinner. I've done some awful things in my life.

I believe You died on the cross to wash away my sins.

Please forgive me.

Please help me live the way You want me to live.

In Jesus Name,

Amen"

I was in fourth grade, or getting ready to go into fourth grade. Young, yes, but I knew right then God was calling me. I felt Him nearby everywhere I went. I still do because I see His hand in every part of the creation.

I'd always felt like an outsider before, but after making this decision, I really felt like a misfit. I was fanciful as a child, with a good imagination, but there was still something, some kind of wall, between me and the other kids I knew, like it was impossible to really connect with them.

This got worse as I got into my teenage years, as you might expect. Those are rough years for anyone. It was a good thing I had my Savior to lean on and the guidance of the Holy Spirit. I wouldn't be here now if it wasn't for Him. I never had an easy time making friends and in 9th grade, I changed schools. I had to make new friends and most of them were Catholic. I loved them, still do, but it was more difficult to connect with that difference in the spiritual doctrine hovering between us. In the middle of that year, I asked my mom to get me out of that school and help me find another one because I felt smothered. But I think back on my time there and I do smile. It was an experience I'm glad I was able to have.

I moved to a new school the following year. It was no easier to make friends and the one friend I made before the school year started, turned out to be a malicious person. The one good friend I made during that year hated me and ignored me after I asked (and was rejected) a friend of mine, who she happened to have a crush on at the time, to attend a banquet with me at my church. I only asked him because I was pushed to do it by a teacher I respected. I would've gone alone like I usually did. No one really paired off at those events anyway. But it was a serious blow to my confidence. At that point, I didn't really try to befriend anyone. My faith was growing, though, and rather than take my life (the thoughts were fleeting but they were there), I stuck it out.

School had always been a drag, though I did well enough in my studies. But church and the youth group were my salvation when it came to socializing. I lived for those moments in Sunday School, Discipleship Training, and youth events. I was part of the cool kids for a little while and it was pretty heady stuff.

Not only did I get to sing with our youth group at church, I got to sing in the choir and the specialty concert choir at school. In doing the latter, I finally made a few friends. Some of them, I still keep in contact with. It was in those moments, chapel, Bible study, youth events, where God was really working on me and convincing me of the certainty of His presence. I still had moments where I knew I was a misfit and an outsider in all those places, but I got to participate in so many things, it wasn't such a big deal.

It was also during my teenage years that I started to doubt my conversion. Some religions teach that you can lose your salvation, but that never made any kind of sense to me. I believed then, and still do, if you have felt the Savior's presence and heard His call, there's no going back. You either respond with a willing heart and mind, or you reject Him utterly. Your life, the decisions you make from that point on will show whether or not your conversion was true. The Bible even says that in Matthew 7:16-18:

You will recognize them by their fruit. Can people pick grapes from thorn bushes, or figs from thistles? Likewise, every healthy tree produces good fruit, but a poor tree produces bad fruit. A healthy tree cannot bear bad fruit, or a poor tree good fruit. - Complete Jewish Bible[1]

I started wondering whether my fruit was good or bad, whether I was right with God for real. I recommitted my life twice over the three years I spent at the prep school. One teacher helped me see clearly that my conversion as a young child was a true conversion, that the moment I heard God's call and responded was the moment I surrendered to Him as Lord over my whole life. I didn't need to be baptised again. I just needed to be sure I was staying connected to Him in prayer and Bible study, and working to follow His commands.

1. https://www.messianicjewish.net/pages/copyright

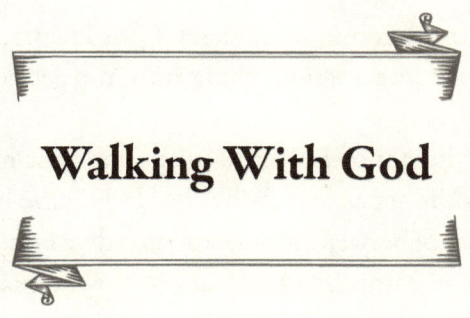

Walking With God

My walk with God has never been what you'd call easy. But neither has it been as difficult as that of Corrie ten Boom, or Saint Peter, or Stephen, or Paul. I'm a pray-er, though. When I pray, it takes time to get everything I want to say out there. My kids dread it when it's my turn to pray at night because they know I just have so much to say. And I don't want to miss anything.

As a child, I used to pray for blue eyes and blonde hair. It's OK. You can laugh if you want to. It's a rather silly prayer, but it was the cry of my heart. I felt my brown hair and green eyes were ugly compared to my gorgeous friends, one of whom had beautiful, long black hair and cool blue eyes, and another who was of German heritage and had sun-gold hair with natural large curls and clear blue eyes. Now, you may laugh at this, but when I got to my second year of high school, one of the older guy students mentioned my eyes, asking what color they were. I said green and he said he'd thought they were blue. I noticed at that point that my eyes change color in different lighting and with different colored shirts. It had probably always been that way, but I never noticed at the right time. My hair is still brown, though sprinkled with lots of gray, but I've learned to love my natural state since then.

Another major thing I prayed for was a boyfriend. I had made it all the way to my senior year of high school without dating anyone. And I knew years before then that I would not be dating anyone in my class or age range, and that I would not be dating anyone I knew while growing up. I don't know how I knew. I just did. We didn't have the same ideals.

We didn't have many common interests. I just knew it wouldn't work. And dating for me was a serious thing from the get-go, never a game. See? Misfit.

God heard the cry of His little misfit and sent my husband. He wasn't interested in me at first. Why should he have been? There's an eight year difference between us. He was already working in the US Air Force and I was still finishing high school. So you may be wondering how that all came about. He was actually working with our youth group and coming to church regularly. He'd made a profession of faith and felt he'd been called into ministry. We hung out within the youth group and that was the extent of our connection. Then it was time for prom and I needed a date. My parents actually suggested I ask him, so I did. We're still together.

But that wasn't easy, either. He came with his own terrible inner struggles which had to be overcome through years and years of battles. God knew I needed him as much as he needed me. God knew I wouldn't give up on him, no matter how painful it was in the process. I was determined.

Through all those ups and downs, God has been faithful. Some of my dear friends say God has never done that for them and they can't really believe in Him. To them, I want to say, God is faithful to the faithful. If you haven't dedicated yourself to living His way, then you can't really expect Him to bless you. I don't expect that from Him.

Want an example? In our faith, we tithe ten percent of our earnings. Anytime I skipped paying tithe because the bills seemed too large to cover, we surely did not have enough to pay for everything. But when I was faithful to pay my tithe, we had an adequate supply of all we needed. Not overmuch, mind you! Just enough to make certain we had what we needed. God is faithful to the faithful.

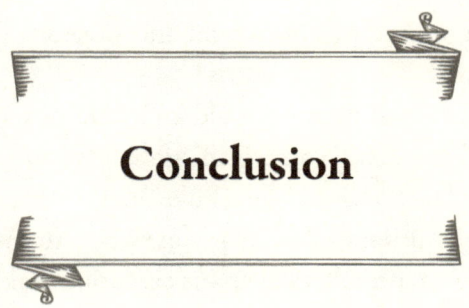

Conclusion

So much more happened to me over the course of my life. It may look easy to you, but I guarantee you my life has been no walk through a rose garden. The one reason I keep pressing on is the thought that one day I will be able to live eternally with God, the Creator of All That Is, with my Savior, the Messiah Yeshua, who rescued me from my sinful self.

When I write, I want to do so in a way that is pleasing to God and pleasant for humankind. I hope I'm doing that and I hope you are enjoying my efforts. God has prepared me for this writing journey. He's filled me with all kinds of knowledge, gleaned from many different experiences throughout my life. More than anything, I want to give back. I've been given so much, I want to share what I have with others who are interested.

So if you read something in this essay that has you wanting to know more about the God I serve, I would like to point you to the book of John[1] in the Bible. It's an excellent place to start and includes some of my favorite verses. Once you've finished there, you might want to take a look at what some call the Romans Road to Salvation[2]. There are several specific scriptures in the book of Romans that teach how a person can begin their own walk with God. I hope you're in the family of God with me. But if not, then I hope you'll take a little time to learn what this is all about. Know that either way, I prayed for you

---

1.   https://www.biblegateway.com/passage/?search=John+1&version=CJB

2.   https://www.biblegateway.com/blog/2022/06/evangelism-the-romans-road-to-salvation/

even before you opened this document and someone cares about your spiritual well-being.

There's one other thing you should know before embarking on this journey. It won't be easy. Nothing in life is easy, after all. Jesus even warned the people who heard him. (Luke 9:23)

Then Yeshua told his talmidim, "If anyone wants to come after me, let him say 'No' to himself, take up his execution-stake, and keep following me." - Complete Jewish Bible[3]

But having God on my side has made the difficult things in life much easier to bear. I don't always understand the why, but I believe God has a plan and it's a good one because He is ultimate good and can be nothing else. Please don't let thoughts of what-ifs and possible future difficulties keep you from experiencing the beauty and love of the Savior who gave all to wash you clean from your sins.

---

3. https://www.messianicjewish.net/pages/copyright

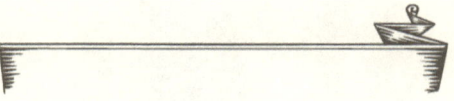

My Prayer for You

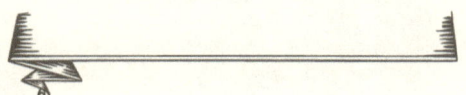

"Dear Heavenly Father,
My prayer for each person who reads this is that You would speak to their hearts.
I pray that you would supply them with what they need.
For those looking for something to fill the void within, I pray that these words will open a door to knowledge of who You really are and what You really offer.
And I pray that You would keep them in the best possible health and safety according to the plan You have for each of their lives.
In the name of Yeshua, the Messiah, I pray.
Amen"

Don't miss out!

Visit the website below and you can sign up to receive emails whenever Robin McElveen publishes a new book. There's no charge and no obligation.

https://books2read.com/r/B-A-LNLG-YANXB

BOOKS 2 READ

Connecting independent readers to independent writers.

Also by Robin McElveen

Children of Y'Dahnndrya
Ripples

Tales of Y'Dahnndrya
The Tale of Outh'n Durr

Watch for more at https://www.authorrobinmcelveen.com/.

About the Author

Robin McElveen is the author of the *Children of Y'Dahnndrya* YA fantasy series, of which *Ripples* is the first tale. She lives in Louisiana with her family. In addition to writing, she enjoys singing and playing music, creating art, and sewing costumes. As a Christian, she tries to keep her books in line with her faith. Faith and family come first. She's taught her children at home since 1998 and feels there's a growing need for quality books which promote good morals. She's doing all she can to help meet that need.

Read more at https://www.authorrobinmcelveen.com/.

About the Publisher

MKRM Author is the exclusive publishing imprint for books by Robin McElveen and Melody Kittles. Find out more here: https://www.authorrobinmcelveen.com

www.ingramcontent.com/pod-product-compliance
Lightning Source LLC
Chambersburg PA
CBHW050858180626
46814CB00007B/2778